The Proposal

The Proposal

BAE MYUNG-HOON

Translated by Stella Kim

Honford Star

This translation first published by Honford Star 2024

Honford Star Ltd.
Profolk, Bank Chambers
Stockport
SK1 1AR
honfordstar.com

Copyright © Bae Myung-hoon
Translation copyright © Stella Kim 2024
Original Korean title: 청혼
All rights reserved
The moral right of the translator and editors has
been asserted.

ISBN (paperback): 978-1-915829-12-2
ISBN (ebook): 978-1-915829-06-1
A catalogue record for this book is available from the British Library.

Printed and bound in Paju, South Korea
Cover illustration by Jisu Choi
Typeset by Honford Star
Cover paper: 250 gsm Vent Nouveau by TAKEO, Japan
Endleaves: 116 gsm NT Rasha by TAKEO, Japan

This book is published with the support of the
Literature Translation Institute of Korea (LTI Korea).

1 3 5 7 9 10 8 6 4 2

Contents

THE PROPOSAL	7
Chapter One	9
Chapter Two	19
Chapter Three	33
Chapter Four	49
Chapter Five	61
Chapter Six	73
Chapter Seven	89
Chapter Eight	99
Chapter Nine	117
Chapter Ten	131
Chapter Eleven	133

So, if I understand you correctly, you're not interested in things like outer space? Because you're exhausted and overwhelmed enough from just trying to survive every day in this world.

I'm sorry, sir, but this spacecraft called Earth you are on is orbiting around the Sun at a speed of thirty kilometers per second. Additionally, this star called the Sun has been hurtling through the outskirts of a galactic system for billions of years at an astonishing speed of 220 kilometers per second. Moreover, this cramped cabin called Seoul, situated near the 37th parallel north of the spacecraft Earth, is revolving around the spacecraft at a speed of about 370 meters per second.

Yet you have never experienced motion sickness, not even once? I believe that means you must be a born astronaut! So please don't say that you are not a spaceman. And stop calling this confined cabin the world.

Now, let me ask you again. Why did you choose to board Earth?

1

Come visit me when you get some time off. The new vacation cruiser began service last month, and I think even you're going to like it. It's for people who want a vacation but can't go all the way to Earth, so apparently there is a lot to do even during a long stay. I haven't been myself yet, but everyone has been making a big fuss about how Earth's gravity has been perfectly recreated on the cruiser. It doesn't seem all that perfect to me, but all Earth-borns seem crazy about it. One of our operations soldiers went on and on about how he wanted to get married there, but between you and me he's never even dated anyone. In any case, it's a rather interesting vessel. Touring the cruiser itself could be fun, too, because of its unique shape.

To start, it has wings. Two adorable little wings, looking cool and carefree as they protrude from both sides of the fuselage, even though they're completely useless since there is no air current to cut through in space. But when you keep looking at them, you begin to wonder if those wings are actually propelling the cruiser forward, rather than the engines. And they look as though they might start flapping really fast in an emergency. They're really cute. The things that Earthians come up with!

But what's more impressive is the pair of vertical wings on the back of the hull. They're ridiculously small compared to the huge nozzle behind them, but the angle—my goodness, the angle—of the wings is fantastic. They look elegant, agile, and even romantic. They're probably the most spectacular things in the entire fleet. That's why it's the most popular photo spot for people who come visit. Apparently, they're going to make a new logo for the fleet based on those tail wings, and I think it's a great idea. I'm sure they will be the most popular attraction in town.

I really like the new cruiser, too. It's the only vessel with a distinction between top and bottom. Ever since the concept designs, every aspect of the cruiser deviates from other vessels in the way it immediately catches your eye. You know how some people say that one thing, one object, can make you see the entire world in a different light? There's no greater compliment to a designer than that, and that's exactly how the cruiser makes me feel. Whenever I look at it, it feels as

The Proposal

though the wild imaginations of people who have never left Earth have become a physical reality and are spreading throughout the entirety of outer space. A bit cheesy to put it like that but intriguing aesthetics, I think.

Earth-borns apparently feel this affection more strongly. They almost feel nostalgia, because it's the outer space that they'd dreamed of as children. Now you know, in a place unaffected by gravity, there is no distinction between up and down. That's the honest truth, but that's not the outer space that people dream of in their childhood. I think that was probably the reason they designed the cruiser this way—to have an obvious top and bottom even at a cursory glance. Top and bottom! Earthians and their silly imaginations.

On what could be called the "topside" of the vessel, two long decks are stretched out like runways, and those are the places where people plant their feet. Similar to land on Earth. The side opposite the decks—what you might refer to as the "underside" of the vessel—is lined with small nozzles that lift the decks upward at the speed of about eight meters per second squared. And by upward, I don't mean an actual "up" but the direction that seems to be up based on the shape of the vessel. The ship gradually gains speed towards that direction. It's far slower than the acceleration at which an object falls on Earth, but it creates a similar sensation to gravity. It'll be much slower after the promotional opening period because it consumes way too much fuel, but that's how artificial gravity is created. Like how you feel a bit heavier when the elevator starts to move.

I'm sorry if I sound like I think Earthians are stupid. But contrary to what you might expect, when the cruiser maintains a fixed speed, people on the decks feel as though they are in zero gravity. They grow anxious, flailing their arms and legs. But when acceleration is at a constant rate, people start to feel as though they are standing on solid ground and their faces become much more relaxed. You know what the cruiser looks like from another spacecraft when it's accelerating? It looks like a free-falling object that is gaining more and more speed, about to burst out somewhere beyond the universe. In the opposite direction than what the people on the decks feel is the bottom.

But no need to worry, because there is no chance for the cruiser to shoot off to the other end of the universe. Not only is it impossible for it to accelerate that fast, but also it flips upside down after some time. The cruiser does half a turn so that its underside, the side with the nozzles, then faces the opposite direction. Once the ship has been fully inverted, the nozzles begin to spew flames again at the same rate of acceleration as before. That way, it gradually slows down. It doesn't start going in the other direction, but rather it continues to go in the same direction as it had been moving, but with a decreasing velocity. That causes negative acceleration, but even then, people on the decks feel the same force of gravity as before. After a while, the velocity becomes zero and the cruiser begins to accelerate again, in the same direction, returning to its original position. Then it flips around once again. It goes back and forth that way, consuming all the fuel it holds.

Doesn't this whole turning upside down remind you of something? The general staff of the fleet call it "wokking." Because when you look at the cruiser from afar, it looks as though some being is sauteing people on the long decks over fire. You can't actually see people inside the cruiser from other ships because it is too far away, but that's what it looks like in the promo video. People going wild while they get sautéed. It's fascinating.

But when you actually stand on the decks, you don't feel the cruiser moving apparently. Except when the cruiser flips over. Instead, you feel a gravitational pull from head to feet, and it makes you think that the whole universe has the same sense of direction as you do. When you stand on the decks and look toward the fleet, apparently it looks as though the fleet is rising and setting over the horizon. A fleet of spacecrafts embroidering the sky instead of stars. Funnily enough, people think it looks romantic. Because the cruiser feels like a cruise ship, floating on the surface of the vast expanse of water called outer space.

Didn't you say that there was a popular theme park ride on Earth that makes you feel like you're in zero gravity? And yet, when Earthians come to space, they get excited about a ride that allows them to experience gravity!

I think what Earth-borns are nuts about is the fact that they can play soccer on the cruiser. It's impossible to create gravity on such a large plane with the artificial gravity you can generate by rotating a vessel. When a round spacecraft is rotated, people feel that the side of the walls where they are standing is the bottom, which means that all walls in the spacecraft are the bottom, and therefore none of them are the "bottom." But on the new cruiser, there is an agreed-upon bottom: the decks. Since dozens of people can stand on the same ground, they can play Earth soccer. Though the gravitational pull is weaker than it is on Earth. By the way, do Earth-borns really love soccer that much? I asked someone once, who told me, "Well, I don't know. It's strange, but I get this desire to play soccer whenever I put my military uniform on." It sounded like a joke, but to be honest, I don't get it.

In any case, Earth-borns are a strange bunch. When they

The Proposal

stand with their two feet on the fake land resembling a frying pan, some people go wild over it to the point they tear up and shout. Saying that it's a blessing to have up and down. Is that right? The most primal ethic that makes humans *human* is not the taboos against cannibalism or incest but the ability to tell apart up from down, apparently. Something about how a human ear must hear the sound of gravity pulling their body long before they can hear the voice of their ego or conscience.

Whenever I'm told things like that, I never know what to say. The first time, I wondered what it meant, but these days, I think of you. That must be how you feel about the world too, right? I remember you saying that you couldn't stand the space sickness you get in outer space because you lose all sense of up and down. I'd heard other people say something similar, but I'd never tried to understand what they were feeling because it wasn't relevant to me. But after I learned that you feel the exact same way, it became relevant to me. I get startled every time I think that that's the kind of world you are living in, that even though we live in the same galaxy, it feels as though we are living in two completely different universes.

It also leads me to think, "Ah, that's why the UES—the United Earth Surface—and the Allied Orbital Forces Command are leery of space-borns like me!"

But that doesn't mean I've come to understand Earth-borns. Why is it that we're not trying to understand each other's universes? There has never been a time when it was as easy as it is now to visit each other's worlds!

You know what still makes me chuckle? That time I visited you on Earth, and I couldn't stand up properly because I couldn't handle the gravity and had to crawl everywhere. On the day we went to the falls with you pushing me on a wheelchair, and your mischievous face as you scolded me rather sternly about how I dared bring so much luggage when I couldn't even handle my own body in the sacred gravisphere of Earth. I did feel like I was an alien. I mean, that was the kind of look Earth-borns gave me. But from my perspective, it was the Earth-borns who were strange. Once, at the Moon Station, I was astonished to see Earth-borns running like they were nearly flying. How strong they were! To people like me, who haven't heard the sound of gravity from birth, Earth-borns seem to have limbs that are much too strong. Do you know what I said upon seeing them at the Moon Station on that day?

"What the heck? They're freaking aliens!"

A world inhabited by such strong people. I loved Earth. Though it was hard to get adjusted. I remember one morning, waking up completely forgetting that I was on Earth and

The Proposal

struggling to push the bed to float to the center of the room as I always did in space. You opened your eyes a slit and let out a quiet chuckle. That face—your face—pops into my head several times a day. The sun pouring into the room. Or perhaps it was rain that was pouring down. I have thought of your beautiful back dozens of times between yesterday and today.

When you get some time off, you must come visit. There's a room with a great view at the hotel on the new cruiser. During the last maneuver training, the chief of staff must have been in a great mood, because he gave out hotel vouchers as prizes. I should be able to rent a room for about 360 hours during peak season. I hope you don't turn me down, and you do come visit for real. To get vouchers for that hotel from Earth, you'd have to be old friends with a former president at minimum. I'll save mine for you.

I saw yesterday that the travel time from Earth to the fleet will be reduced to 130 hours. I heard how terrible 130 hours of space sickness can be for Earthians from an intelligence officer in the Inspection Force who recently arrived here from Earth. What with zero gravity and high-speed space travel. But once this combat comes to an end, our fleet will be stationed much closer to Earth, though I can't tell you the details.

Once this battle is over, when this war is over, I plan to take dance classes on the new cruiser. If I learn to dance like they do on Earth, perhaps Earth-borns would be willing to understand me better.

2

Yesterday, I received a summons from the Inspection Force Command. I reported to the chief of staff and went to the Command Module, and they told me to write up a statement of reasons. The new cruiser that I mentioned in the previous letter actually came attached to this newly stationed Inspection Force. In fact, the cruiser is named the *Liddell* after the Inspection Force commander. Anyway, our working conditions have gotten intense since the Inspection Force began their work. I mean, sure, I've been through a few operational readiness inspections in my time, but I always thought they were just to tick boxes on some document. Yet within a single month there's been at least three times more inspections than I have ever received in my life. So when I was told to submit a statement of reasons, I had no idea for what since I didn't know what they found on me. Seeing as how the Inspection Force is tightening the reins, I think this war is going to last longer than I had expected.

The official position of the Allied Orbital Forces is still that they will not prolong the fight. But who are they to say? If they had the ability to end the war swiftly, then why didn't they do so a generation ago? Why did the UES go beyond creating a political coalition and establish a joint military organization called the Allied Orbital Forces? It's evident that no one can predict the outcome of combat in space like this. Because no one has ever had any previous experience in this area.

I know that many people out there think that the UES Government knows something. Not just on Earth but here in space too. People who believe rumors, like how the enemy fleet may also be human made. But I don't think so. Because there is no way Earth had the resources to build another colossal fleet like this. Earthians couldn't *not* notice if such commodities and supplies were diverted to space. See how impoverished Earth became building this fleet. If there were two of these fleets, Earth would be twice as poor now. So if there was another manmade fleet, ordinary people would've been the first to know, rather than the intelligence authorities.

The enemy must be an alien fleet. The problem is not that the UES is trying to hide something. It'd be a relief to know that they have something to hide. The real problem is that not even they know what is going on—that they don't even have information to hide. I hope that some of them have a clear understanding of the current situation, even if that information remains sealed and no one ever finds out. If I had some kind of assurance about that, I wouldn't be so anxious.

I wonder where they came from. Could they really have come through an interdimensional portal? These days, I think it makes sense that more and more people are taking out and reading the copies of *Prophecies* they'd stuffed into their closets, because there are too many inexplicable events. Some time ago, I was briefly in Fleet Commander General De Nada's office, and even he had *Prophecies* on his shelf! General De Nada, of all people! It must have been the copy that was issued to him when he first enlisted. It was made of quality material. Granted it looked old, but untouched. When he saw me glancing at it, he said, "The Allied Orbital Forces Headquarters brought it out again. Looks like people who believe in the interdimensional portal, the so-called "Temple of Doom," have crawled out of whatever rock they've been living under. I wouldn't be surprised if they eventually force you lower rank officers to memorize several verses. Might even make us recite them before the Inspection Force. I've heard that there's a revised edition; some of the content is different from when I had to memorize it. Are prophecies usually revised and updated?"

"It must be a different translation."

I knew that a revised edition had been published, but this was the first time I heard about the changing power dynamics in the Allied Orbital Forces. The prophecy enforcers holding all the chips. I thought they'd been thrown out a long time ago.

I'm not saying that I take the UES Council's insight lightly. It was no ordinary feat to decide to build such a colossal fleet in the quiet outer space without any sign of threat. The initiative was even more impressive than the decision itself. Had the plan failed, everyone would've lost their jobs—some, their lives. They couldn't have done it without considerable conviction. Sure, there was *Prophecies*, but that only predicted events of the next decade, and nothing about the following thirty years was right. Where in that iffy book could they have possibly gained such confidence? What could have fueled the madness of squeezing out such an astronomical sum to be spent on building an unprecedented and unparalleled fleet? For twenty-five years at that.

It couldn't have been just madness. It's clear there must have been leadership and insight involved, enough to keep the government standing even after spending so much on the fleet. I mean, it took thirty years—until the moment the enemy finally appeared and everything in *Prophecies*, which people had concluded was false, turned out to be delayed truths. Was there ever a prophet who was more credible than *Prophecies*? I don't know exactly what, but I believe that they had something. But I disagree with the idea that everyone needs to read *Prophecies*. That's not right. The universe that we are living in is clearly different from the stories in *Prophecies*.

Whatever my opinions are, the official stance of the Allied Orbital Forces Command is that the war is guaranteed to come to a swift end. I don't know if they actually believe that. It's probably their hope, rather than a prediction. Seeing as how the Inspection Force are here, doing whatever they are doing, it seems that the war is going to be drawn out. The fact that they are tightening their grip around us means that something has been loosened, out of control, somewhere else.

To be fair, the Inspection Force couldn't leave us be. Because of the tremendous sum of money—an amount that would've started a massive revolt on Earth had the enemy appeared merely two years later—that flowed into the Allied Orbital Forces. They had to show that all that money went into something, so they were forced to do something. On Earth, there was an endless string of conspiracy theories about whether the money had actually been spent on building a fleet and whether the fleet was a "ghost fleet," built only on paper to line the pockets of several high-ranking officials, rather than an actual one consisting of spacecrafts in outer space. But it's a fact that we are here, now. This "ghost fleet" that I am a member of isn't in the pockets of the UES Council members but a physical asset floating in the solar system, and it has the potential do so much more than we anticipated. Think about it. Even if we got together all the means of violence that humanity had ever previously invented, they would not last five minutes against our fleet. But no one on our fleet had thought long enough about the power of our fleet to see that.

The Inspection Force saw it though. I mean the people who created the Inspection Force and sent them here. They realized that if our fleet idled in space without anything to do, the fleet's guns might eventually point to Earth. That's why they launched a preemptive attack on our fleet—threw the bomb of inspection on us. We did return fire, but the only thing we could fire back at them was piles of statements of reasons.

When I was first told to write up a statement of reasons, I felt like I was drafting a report of my mistakes. While writing, I was overcome with a sense of shame, thinking that I'd never imagined myself to be such a flawed person. But as time passed, I had to write a statement nearly every day, and I started to not think much of it. At some point, I made a standard template for a statement of reasons and just filled out the date, relevant provisions, and my violations. It seemed that no one really cared. Looking through all those statements of reasons would be a lot of work. But yesterday, I was summoned. Told to visit the Inspection Force Command in person to write up the statement. Had I done something that was particularly wrong? I couldn't even guess what it was. So I asked.

The inspection officer said, "They tell me you're the commander of the Rebel Force."

I let go of my pen in midair and looked up. People often do that in places where gravity doesn't work. I think that might have rubbed him the wrong way, because the inspection officer's face hardened a bit.

"I am, but …"

"Write that."

"But it was just a joke, sir."

"I know. You think you'd be relaxedly sitting here writing a statement of reasons if I didn't know that it was just a joke?"

But the thing is, the "Rebel Force" is just a social club. The name of a group of the fleet's operations officers. We just get together and hit the bottle. I couldn't believe that something like this would get us in trouble.

I submitted my statement of reasons and went to the General Staff Office to report my whereabouts, and the chief of staff said to me, "No wonder. The Inspection Force Commander thinks this fleet is like the Marine Corps, when nothing could be further from the truth. This is why I said we shouldn't refer to spacecrafts as ships. And to not use the word 'fleet.'"

"Is this fleet the Marine Corps? What is the Marine Corps?"

"The Marine Corps is, well, a dispatch force. Though originally, it was a landing force. Back in the day, during the Earth era, there was an empire whose primary offensive force was the Navy, while for most other countries it was the Army. It was called the United Kingdom. It was an island country. The country itself was made up of islands, but they also crisscrossed all over the Earth's oceans with their ships. The troops dispatched from the empire had to cross the oceans on ships to get to the colonies or conflict areas. So, their landing force had to be the overseas dispatch force. The country that inherited hegemony from the United Kingdom was the United States of America, and apparently their major overseas dispatch force was also the Marines."

"Okay," I said. "But how is that related to this?"

"Have you ever seen the Marine Corps? Do you even know what they're like?"

The Proposal

"You said they were a landing force."

"They are, but I'm saying, the military branch employed as the primary offensive force in war has to undergo rigorous training and endure strict discipline when they're not landing anywhere. Even after completing their military service, the Marines used to maintain the same hierarchy they had during their service in civilian life. Here, we're not like that at all, as you know. I mean, look at the way you're standing in front of your superior."

"What did I do?"

"Hey, you should at least ... never mind. Forget it. In any case, he misjudged. General Liddell, he's a 17th Military School graduate. So, he didn't quite get the hang of how things are here. Don't get me wrong, he's a smart man. But we're definitely not the Marines."

"Then what are we?"

"We're the Air Force. Obviously."

"The Air Force?"

"Sure! There was a time when the military force in charge of everything between the land's surface and the outermost reaches of the atmosphere was classified as the Air Force. Though all of that is now under the jurisdiction of the Allied Orbital Forces. In any event, that was what we were. The very first Space Force was established in the United States, branching out from the Air Force. And when it was temporarily abolished, it was reintegrated into the Air Force. You know, the Air Force emphasized flexibility a little more, over discipline. Possibly because there was no hand-to-hand combat in the Air Force, and people all just fought via machines. There was this joke—a Marine Corps commander meets with an Air Force commander and brags about the bravery of his special unit. He says, 'I gave them an order to eliminate a target, and while crossing the ocean to eliminate the target they killed seven sharks with their bare hands.' Hearing that, the Air Force commander issues the same order to the special Air Force unit to eliminate the target and kill seven sharks with their bare hands. Then thirty minutes later, one of his subordinates comes to him and tells him that they can't do it. 'Why would you ask us to do that?' the subordinate asks. After sending him away, the Air Force commander turns to the Marine commander and says, 'Isn't he, in fact, the definition of bravery? Because true courage is the courage to say no to what can't be done.' So, what do you think? Do you think this fleet is closer to the Marine Corps or the Air Force?"

The chief of staff asked me this with a triumphant look on his face for some reason. I'm sure the answer was probably the latter. And we must have seemed much worse than the Air Force. From the Inspection Force's General Liddell's perspective, I

The Proposal

mean. I don't know why, but it was apparently inconceivable that a group of operations officers, whether in the Air Force or the Army or other military forces that used to be on the Earth's surface, name their social club the Rebel Force.

"So is that why the inspection officer tried to wring something out of me until I bled dry?" I asked.

"Right. And you wouldn't know this, because why would you, but that statement of reasons you said you'd just written and submitted? It won't do much to you, but it won't be great for the commander, I think you've just thrown a wrench in General De Nada's career."

Just as he said, when the Inspection Force's report was delivered to Earth, there was a big solar storm of blowback from the Allied Orbital Forces Headquarters. Apparently, they went berserk when they found out that there was a private group called the Rebel Force in the armed forces. I honestly don't know what all the fuss was about. Why is it that the military has stricter discipline for rearguard units than frontline troops?

In conclusion, though, I inadvertently succeeded in orchestrating a revolt. As written in the *Code of Revolt*, I ended up forcing General De Nada out of his position as the commander, albeit for a short while. The commander of the Inspection Force took over as the acting commander of the fleet, and looking back on it now, I can't help but wonder if that was why they sent the Inspection Force from the start. After all, they didn't dispatch the "Inspection Unit" but the "Inspection Force"—an elite subdivision consisting of vessels that were better performing and newer than our entire fleet, though smaller in number.

But trouble brings trouble, as they say. Had the UES not gone to that extreme, the general would never have realized the importance of his position. You can see it from his name, De Nada. It's not his real name, but rather a nom de guerre. In the military, we call it a "call sign," and everyone just calls him that. The same goes for General Liddell. Liddell is a call sign he took from the military theorist Liddell Hart.

De Nada might sound to you like the name of some fancy aristocratic family, but it actually means "of nothing." An aristocratic surname would have the name of his domain after "De," but instead he has "Nada," which means "nothing." It means he has no land to rule. Doesn't it sound like an oath by him to own nothing in life? But the UES didn't believe him. Because although he had no domain, he had the military—a force big enough to subdue all humanity within seconds. And soon enough, people viewed De Nada as wanting to be the owner of the place that had "nothing"—meaning the vast, empty outer space.

The Proposal

"It's not like I insisted on coming here. They were the ones who deployed me, so why the hell are they suspicious of me now?"

Apparently that was what General De Nada said when he was informed that some of his commanding privileges were to be revoked while the Inspection Force conducted additional investigations.

I'm sure it was then. It was then that his heart began to stir.

3

Most people call it the Buggler Paradox, but engineers first called it the Boozer's Paradox. The name sounds like a phenomenon discovered by someone named Buggler, but Buggler was just some engineer who had a passionate, soul-consuming devotion to booze. His colleague discovered the phenomenon and first thought of the name Boozer's Paradox, so he jokingly started calling it the Buggler Paradox, and that name caught on apparently.

This Buggler Paradox was the lesson we learned from our very first combat with the enemy. Before the first combat took place, not many people thought we'd lose. Not just because of the fleet—our fleet is, I mean, an amazing fleet—but, above all, because of our main armament, the L-22. The twenty-second version of the weapon that shoots at light speed particles named after the Devil, Lucifer, the light-bringer. Anyone who's seen Lucifer particles obliterate a target in space would know right away that we had an absolute weapon that could immediately overpower any alien enemy. It was literally an absolute weapon, where "absolute" meant that we wouldn't need to develop a twenty-third version of the weapon for a long while. For at least two hundred years.

But that belief shattered in the first combat. This vicious, ultimate weapon turned out to be utterly useless in actual fighting because our aim was beyond appalling.

Thirty seconds at the speed of light—combat began when the distance between us and the enemy was thirty light-seconds. Their preemptive attack destroyed seventeen of our expensive warships, so we weren't exactly in the mindset to make attempts at conversation. We had no choice but to respond in kind. We began retaliating exactly two minutes after the enemy's initial attack. And do you know how many enemy ships we destroyed in the next half an hour? A grand total of one. That's when it became glaringly apparent that we would never succeed at taking aimed shots and hitting targets at this distance.

It takes thirty seconds minimum for our detectors to identify the precise location of an enemy that is thirty light-seconds away. If we process the information instantaneously, that is. And even if we can respond without delay and shoot at them right away, it takes another thirty seconds for our

L-22 beam to reach the target because Lucifer particles also travel at light speed, which is like the universe's speed limit. This means that it takes a total of one full minute for our response fire to reach the enemy. But there is no guarantee the enemy ship will be in precisely that location by that time. And to top it all off, it then takes another thirty seconds to identify if our attack was successful. Whether we use optical signals or radio signals, we have to wait until we receive that information coming in at light speed.

Plus, even when their formation appeared to be stationary, each ship in the enemy fleet was teetering and wobbling, as though they were being driven by some drunk pilot. That's what they looked like. Shaking, or trembling. Whatever it was, the point is that they were not in the same position they had been in a minute earlier. Since we had no prior experience with space combat, there was no way for us to know what strategy to deploy. In that very first battle, we began returning fire while remaining in the same spot or moving in a way that could be easily predicted by the enemy. Had we continued with that plan, it would've been a matter of time before we were decimated. All in all, we were extremely lucky that they didn't want to continue the fight. It would have led to our annihilation.

What piqued my curiosity the most was just that—why

did they stop attacking us then? Perhaps they didn't mean to engage us in a full-fledged battle yet. Or perhaps they thought we'd set a trap and were waiting for them to make a move.

We eventually found out the reason. Their problem was the Buggler Maneuver. Even when a fleet is stationary, each ship has to jet gas in all directions—left and right, up and down—and that requires too much fuel. Additionally, when a ship keeps on jetting gas that way, its body heats up more quickly. So while we were in a crisis, the enemy was about to explode as well. That was the tentative conclusion of our general staff.

They say General De Nada's greatest achievement so far is plastering nozzles all over the ships so that we can also "drunken maneuver" our fleet. Because these modifications couldn't be done with just an order. The Allied Orbital Forces Headquarters had to approve the budget first, which meant that there were politics involved. It was no easy feat. But in my opinion, his greatest achievement was to boldly let us go on vacation during that time.

"You'll be spending your next vacation in hell, so for now go conquer the Earth."

Isn't he impressive?

As soon as I received my precious vacation days, which could possibly be the very last days I ever get off, I flew 170

The Proposal

hours to spend 40 hours with you and flew back 180 hours to get back on duty. At the time, you asked me if I regretted doing that. I don't. And I would do the same if I get time off again.

"I missed you," I said, and you answered, "Me too."

The exchange took less than a second, and to me that moment was the definition of happiness. Right now, even if I answer your "I love you" right away, it takes seventeen minutes and forty-four seconds for my response to reach you, and it takes another seventeen minutes and forty-four seconds for your response to come to me. Do you know what I find the most stifling about this distance? It's the frustration that comes from not knowing what is happening within that brief period of time between my talking to you and you responding to me.

Even before our first battle with the enemy fleet, people here already knew about the Boozer's Paradox. They knew that after thirty-five minutes and twenty-eight seconds, the heart of your missed one would not be in the same place as before. And it would take another seventeen minutes and forty-four seconds to learn that their heart was elsewhere. That was what made us incessantly anxious. Perhaps that was how General De Nada's daring vacation strategy came to be.

There was only one way for me to get a perfect aim at your heart—to close the distance between us and get to a place where the Boozer's Paradox does not apply. When the thought came to me, I put it into action. And I said to you, "I love you." If it took me another thirty-five minutes and twenty-eight seconds to see the reaction on your face, I might have been wrung dry and withered to death. But with only a short distance between us, there was no chance that I would miss it.

But you know, you kept on misunderstanding what I was trying to say.

"I got it," you said. "Like I said, I love you, too."

"No, no, that's not what I mean."

"What do you want then? You want me to rip my heart out and show you?"

When you said that, I stared at you for a long time in silence. I was hesitant at the time because I didn't know how to express what I had in mind, but what I wanted to say was this—I don't just love you; I love you as much as the distance I flew to see you; my love for you is as wide as this tediously vast universe. And that I wanted to keep you bound to me. But I couldn't say those things. Because I didn't know whether keeping you tethered to me was the right thing to do. I wasn't really sure. So I couldn't say that to you. It wasn't something that I could convey even if I traveled so far to you and eliminated the Buggler Paradox. Because it was a matter of the heart.

The Proposal

After we parted, I flew 180 hours back to the fleet, thinking that it was a shame that I had to spend this vacation traveling for the most part, and guess what I found. Our warships were all looking like drunks! Seeing that, the chief of staff said, "Geez, how much did you give them to drink?"

The improvement project was probably much more haphazard than we'd ever thought. To make the ships' movements more erratic, like butterflies flitting without a set pattern, we had to affix nozzles on all sides of the ships. But since there was no time to redesign and manufacture new ships, they'd literally just turned the ships into patchworks. It was fun to look at though. The ships' designs remained the same in essence, with the only difference being that they now seemed to be adorned with ornaments spewing colorful lights. A Christmas fleet. Like a teeter-tottering mob of wasted Santa Clauses.

That wasn't just a metaphor, because a lot of the people hit the bottle in the aftermath of General De Nada's vacation operation. Most had troubles in their romantic relationships. Reflecting on that, I suppose I could understand the reason the UES sent the Inspection Force to our fleet. Actually, it makes perfect sense. The essence of the problems that the UES and we face lies in "distance"—this physical barrier that is hard to overcome no matter how much we try. That tremendous distance between our fleet and Earth. It doesn't look like much when written on paper, but that daunting gap had appeared insurmountable for all of humanity even a few decades earlier.

We felt the same as the UES did. Being stationed here in space, those of us in relationships desperately wanted to send an inspection force that represented us to Earth as well. We wanted to ask all kinds of questions to confirm whatever was going on and draft up some kind of document on our relationships. I mean, if I learned that you and your friends decided to call your lunch meetings the "Flirtatious Girls' Club," I would've gotten upset just as the Inspection Force did about our "Rebel Force."

And that was probably why I couldn't say those words to you that day, when we were together. Because it was an obsession. Saying that since I flew all this way to see you, my love for you is as tremendous as the distance I traveled to be with you, and therefore you should return the same amount of love to me. That's not something you should ever say to anyone.

Yet unfortunately, more than a few people from the fleet had gone to Earth and said that out loud. Both men and women. The outcome was obviously tragic. So the fleet brimmed with drunks until General De Nada issued a

The Proposal

two-week drinking ban across the entire fleet. I mean, talk about Temple of Doom-ed relationships. One day, when General De Nada found an operations officer drunk and wobbling around her dorm room, apparently he said to her, "I told you to make the ships perform the Buggler Maneuver. When have I instructed you to personally perform such unpredictable deviations?"

Luckily, I didn't tell you to prove that you love me as much as I love you, and thus I managed to keep a more or less clear state of mind upon my return to the fleet. That naturally caught General De Nada's attention.

"You seem like you're in your right mind."

That was what General De Nada said before he appointed me—the leader of the Rebel Force, who were apparently acting to take him down—as a staff officer. At the time, I had no inkling whatsoever that the Inspection Force would show up eventually and make a big deal over our social gathering. Since the Inspection Force crossed the universe to reach our fleet, it became harder and harder to see romance in this war. I think we'd become more like the Marines, even if the transformation was much slower than Earth expected. I wasn't happy about the change.

About two months after Inspection Force Commander Liddell took over part of the peacetime operational command, the second combat—and the first real skirmish—transpired. Initially, everything went as we expected. This time it wasn't only our offensive tactics that failed; the enemy's attacks were also largely ineffective against us. So it could be said to have been a partial success, but that was not how it felt to those in the fleet. Think about it. We were on teetering ships aiming to create absolute chaos without a set pattern of movements. As soon as the Buggler Maneuver began, we started feeling motion sickness. And because the entire plan had been put together in a rush, the devices installed to minimize the queasiness barely worked. It really felt like we were working on the operation while plastered. As though we'd been possessed by the spirit of Mr. Buggler himself. But of course, Mr. Buggler was still alive and kicking then.

About fifteen minutes into the maneuver, it crossed my mind that I might end up dead without even experiencing a real attack. As an operations officer, though, I had an overall positive assessment of the situation. While we couldn't destroy the enemy, we also didn't just sit and watch our own ships get destroyed, which meant that at least we were even. It felt like a small victory. The main goal was to survive for now—you had to be alive to think about strategies and tactics.

The Proposal

In the meantime, however, we became aware of a critical issue. The enemy's shots were getting less frequent, but they were becoming more precise. It wasn't sniping per se, but the shots were growing markedly more accurate. Sure, they were probably making efforts to increase the precision and accuracy of their shots—as soldiers we're always trying to improve our aim. But it was odd, you see. Regardless of how sick we were from being on a rocking ship, the machines were making accurate, aimed shots, and it wasn't as if the Lucifer particles they were shooting at light speed were deviating from their trajectories. The Buggler Paradox was something we thought could guarantee our safety. To avoid beams of Lucifer particles, we had no other choice but to stand behind the barrier of tremendous distance between us and the enemy. And we thought that was a principle that we could always trust. But still, it did happen—some of our ships were destroyed by the enemy's precision fire.

By the time the enemy retreated that day, we'd lost 117 of our warships and suffered a staggering 49,253 casualties. We did have 2,747 more warships, so it wasn't a complete loss, but we couldn't deny that it was a significant blow. The assessment of those who were directly involved in the combat that day was much harsher though. It is mostly remembered as a complete defeat, largely due to the dreadful motion sickness we suffered from the unrefined Buggler Maneuver. A lot of us still remember that day as the day the entire fleet had been on the brink of annihilation.

The first thing that General Liddell did, as soon as we regrouped from the defeat, was to improve the devices that cushioned the effects of the Buggler Maneuver. At the same time, General De Nada assigned a special task to the general staff to identify the reasons behind the Buggler Maneuver's failure to prevent such significant losses.

Immediately, people focused their attention on the prophecies. I mean, think about it. There was absolutely no way to figure out what the enemy's position would be, located thirty light-seconds away, four minutes from now. To do so would be the exact definition of "prophecy."

"What are you saying?" asked Chief of Staff Say More (Say More isn't his call sign, it's a nickname we gave him because he never stops talking), looking perplexed. "They have a prophet or something on each of their ships?"

But he probably knew the answer himself. That the existence of our fleet itself was indisputable proof of the prophet's foresight. Had the Prophet not prophesized or had his prophecy not come true, we wouldn't even be here in the first place. Because this war was something beyond the realms of our wildest dreams.

The Proposal

"That's a problem," remarked General De Nada when he heard our report. "The Prophet lovers are going to rave again, and Liddell's ego will go through the roof. I don't want to see that. Check and see if there could be any other possibilities. If we can't find something else, we have no choice but to advance to a place where the Buggler Paradox doesn't apply and engage in head-to-head combat next time, whether it will work or not. I really hate close combat."

Then he turned to look at me. As a sign that I should take on the responsibility.

"Me, sir?"

"Yes, you."

"My opinion is that it would be better for us to engage in head-to-head combat. If there is no Buggler Paradox, there would be no motion sickness, which would lead to higher morale. Although, I am, or I was, since I was dismissed, the commander of the Rebel Force …"

"Oh you Air Force kids, you never just say 'Yes, sir,' and do what you're told. You, did you say you were space-born?"

I did owe him one, so I had to obey his order. Why did I owe him one? You know, the whole Rebel Force thing. That wasn't an insignificant debt. What else could I do? So, I started gathering people together. Astronomers, mathematicians, physicists. I had them examine the warships that had been shot down by the enemy, and they detected purgatory particle reactions. Meaning, Lucifer particles passed through them. It was proof that Lucifer particles were the most universal and absolute weapons in space, and that our enemy was armed with weapons that were essentially the same as ours.

Ultimately it was the mathematicians who found out what had gone wrong in that second battle. They identified an error in the Buggler Maneuver program installed on our ships. Simply put, the program should have ensured that no discernible pattern or order was created in our ships' movements during the Buggler Maneuver. It strove to create a semblance of chaos, as infinitely close as possible. That was where the glitch was. Because if you had enough time to observe and track our movements with a good enough calculator, you could discern a pattern. The problem on our end was the level of technology we had. They said it would take at least a month to calculate the enemy's movements and find a pattern. We might as well be dead by the time we could get our hands on that data.

On the other hand, when we used all the research data compiled by our mathematicians and calculated the movements of our ships, we found predictable patterns in exactly five minutes. Turns out, our patterns were that simple.

The Proposal

During a mock maneuver session, I ambushed a virtual fleet led by General Liddell's assistant chief of staff for operations and destroyed all 270 of his ships before disappearing into the dark without losing a single ship under my charge. The only difference was the pattern. The program I had was exactly a month more advanced than what they had.

The moment the outcome became clear, General De Nada turned to General Liddell and said, "These days, even the Rebel Force is clever enough to defeat our fleet."

This meant that the reason for our defeat wasn't prophecies. It also meant that I proved to be more useful than he thought.

I became a celebrity after that because the *Prophecies* memorization oral tests were then all cancelled. Instead, everyone had to work on creating more precise chaos, and it seemed that people enjoyed making chaos more than memorizing *Prophecies*. On top of that, we did get better calculators from Earth too.

"How much better is 'better'? Didn't we have one in our fleet?"

I asked a maintenance officer I knew, and she answered, "Of course we didn't have one. That's how it is for computers on spacecrafts. They're ridiculously old fashioned. Compared to computers, spaceships are machines that are in use for a long, long time. Computers, on the other hand, become junk in several months. But these new machines are artificial intelligence. Not a word we can use to describe a mediocre operations officer. Intelligent, I mean. Anyway, let me tell you how amazing these new calculators are. If they had access to a few of your operations briefings, they could predict the consonant of the thirty-fourth syllable that you'd use in your briefing the next day."

"No way."

"Wanna bet?"

I'd forgotten about that conversation for a while. Then, one day, after all the preparations for a more stable Buggler Maneuver were complete, on the morning of the eighth day since the new program began computing the data, that maintenance officer predicted the consonant of the thirty-fourth syllable that came out of my mouth in my briefing. It seemed that everyone had heard what it was going to be except for me. And I did begin the thirty-fourth syllable with that exact consonant.

Upon receiving a sealed envelope that contained the prediction and confirming it was correct by watching the video recording of my briefing, I went straight to General De Nada and said, "I think we're ready to try and take them on."

4

I must have told you this once. People call spaceships "ships," but in space, ships don't sink tragically as they do in the ocean. They might be destroyed when attacked, but they don't sink into the deep, dark sea. Even if the engines fail or the fuel is depleted, ships remain in place rather than disappear. But actually, that's not entirely accurate. Even on regular days, we are submerged in a corner of the deep abyss of outer space. Like a submarine without a single window.

They call it a fleet, but even the closest ship to the one I'm on is about the distance of Earth's radius away. It's a titanic vessel, but at that distance it's no bigger than a tiny star. Similar to the size of Polaris seen from the wreckage of a ship without a helm, the distance renders us as nothing more than stars to each other. And if we turn off the lights and hide behind the darkness by positioning the ship at an angle where sunlight won't reflect off the ship's exterior, it'd be hard for them to tell that there's a vessel here. On top of that, when the new cruiser that has been lit up for months on end, wasting away a tremendous amount of fuel, stops its engines to prevent exposing our location, and the entire fleet minimizes heat emissions to prevent radio signal leaks, then this place truly becomes a submarine.

Well, for some, it's probably more claustrophobic here than on a submarine. Particularly so for Earth-borns. At least in the ocean, they can feel which way the gravity pulls—that sound of Earth they love so much. Of course, that means nothing to people like me or General De Nada who are first-generation space-borns.

The third combat was different from the previous two. We didn't sit and wait for the enemy to appear before us. Instead, we set a trap for them and bided our time for a chance to counterattack. That was the only thing we could do, I mean. Because we had no idea where the enemy was. But there was one thing that worked to our advantage. We knew nothing about the enemy's identity, where they came from, or why they were attacking us, but we knew they would be targeting our fleet. Which meant that at least we could choose where the fight would take place.

"According to *Prophecies*, the Prophet saw the enemy fleet but not much else," said General Say More, the chief of staff.

The Proposal

"He said they would come with spaceships like the ones they had and attack in a way they've been attacking us, coming to us through an interdimensional portal. He was no military expert, so he probably couldn't notice the details, like that they were performing the Buggler Maneuver. And even if he were an expert, he probably couldn't tell what was what with the knowledge that was available at the time. Anyway, he must have thought that since he saw a huge fleet, we should make something similar. It's a logical solution. And a wiser one than what the UES people thought at the time."

The way he said the last sentence, it was like he was pleading for one of us to ask why it was a wiser solution.

Eventually I gave in and bit. "How so?"

"Want to know? Well, you see, it was sort of a large-scale baiting strategy. In the disasters that came before, the target was always Earth. It's the planet with the largest population, and it was the most bustling place around this part of the galaxy, you know. But now, we have this enormous fleet in space. If you were looking at us humans from the outside, where would you assume the center of gravity of the human civilization was? Earth or this fleet?"

"Wouldn't it still be Earth?"

"No, no. Even the UES Allied Orbital Forces Command is suspicious that the center of gravity of humanity has shifted this way. Why else would they have sent the Inspection Force? So, how do you think it looks to people who have no connection whatsoever to Earth? For anyone who comes flying all the way here with such a gigantic fleet, we're definitely the strategic target. All this goes to show that if you launch a fleet like ours in space, at minimum, you eliminate Earth from a list of direct targets. That's what that Prophet man had in mind."

Not everyone agreed with Chief of Staff Say More's assessment, but everyone agreed that the enemy would come find us again. They had done twice already. So we lay quietly in hiding, behind the enormous curtain of space, in a formation ready for counterattack.

Then one day.

"Looks like your love life isn't going very well these days."

Out of the blue, General De Nada addressed me in a voice dripping with boredom, sounding as though he didn't care for an answer.

"Oh, yeah, well, she hasn't been writing back as often," I answered. "These few weeks, all operations officers are refraining from engaging in private communication to prevent intelligence leaks."

"Who told you to do that?"

"Well, if I knew, I'd be annoyed at the person who issued

The Proposal

the directive, but I can't really complain to anyone because it's as good as an order we gave ourselves. It did go out under your name, commander."

"Me? So what's everyone doing now? At the bar hitting the bottle?"

"Well, now, since they can't send video messages, they're just writing letters they can't send, because they'd then be summoned by the Inspection Force. I don't think looking through letters was officially part of the inspection, but it seems that they're now claiming that going through even private messages is a requirement of the operational readiness inspection."

"Hmm, I see."

"What about you, commander? How are you doing?"

"Me? I'm just waiting here to greet the guests, since they're coming all the way here to see me."

He meant the aliens attacking us, I think.

When he said those words though—that they were coming, and he was going to greet them—it gave me a funny feeling. These beings from outer space were coming from all the way across this infinite universe to reach us, whether it was to invade us or whatever. My question was, why? Why were they doing that? And moreover, how? How could they do it?

I feel like a castaway in outer space because the area we

take up is minuscule compared to the expansive emptiness of our surroundings. Just a single spaceship in an area the size of the entire Earth. Alone in a space the size of a planet—an area the size of what could be the entire universe to some people. That is the definition of being stranded. Submerged in the abyss of something. Something dark, silent, boundless, and daunting.

It's hard for me to pinpoint exactly what I mean. Because that *something* is literally nothing. Something that does not exist. The very fact that nothing exists.

In 6,400 kilometers. For nothing to exist in a distance the equivalent of Earth's radius. On the surface of a planet, someone who gets cast adrift in the ocean a mere kilometer away from the coast would float alone until he meets a lonely demise. Here, we're submerged deep inside a corner of the universe, 6,400 kilometers away from any living organism, without even water to envelop us. Beyond 6,400 kilometers is another dot of a spaceship and then again stretches of thousands of kilometers of nothing. And beyond that is another stretch of inconceivably vast empty space. It's a wall. The state of absolute isolation: being unable to reach a place even though there is nothing in your path.

Imagine standing in a huge room. A wide-open room without a single pillar. You can see the walls at the ends of

The Proposal

the room, but the actual distance to each wall is millions of kilometers. You are standing in the middle of that room. Normally, the fact that you can see everything around you without anything blocking your view means you can relax. Because nothing can jump out and ambush you. But not in this room. Even if you are viewing something only thirty light-seconds away, you can't be certain that what you are seeing is what actually exists at that moment. Even if a massive explosion that swept through the entire room were to take place thirty light-seconds away from you, you can't know until after thirty seconds have passed. If there's a predator waiting to pounce on you, it doesn't need to hide somewhere; it can hide itself behind the wall of time and space. What you are seeing isn't the truth. The farther you are from what you are seeing, the more distorted it gets, and even if you are carefully scrutinizing your surroundings, eventually there comes a moment when nothing that you see feels like the truth.

Thirty seconds at the speed of light. Can you imagine how far that distance is? That wall of distance is so thick that we feel hopeless and suffocated, as though we are trapped in a shipwreck submerged hundreds of meters deep under water. Even though we can see everything around us clearly, this thick, solid wall of nothingness distorts any and every event and presence beyond it, just as water distorts the shape of objects. We are waiting for the enemy to appear from behind that wall. These unidentified aliens who are coming all the way across the universe, passing through a wall of time and space that spans a much greater distance than thirty light-seconds.

And the Lucifer particles that can penetrate the thickest hulls in the blink of an eye!

I was staring absently at the screen showing the front view of the fleet when a beam of light from an unidentified source flashed across my eyes. Then the alarms went off. It was the purgatory particle detection alarm. The alarm alerted us that Lucifer particles just passed us by. It must have been a miss. Thank goodness. Had it hit us, we would not be alive. At the same time, we received a report that the enemy fleet had appeared out of thin air at a distance of 47.52 light-seconds and opened fire. Right from the location where the light had flashed.

They found us. Cold sweat ran down my back. I almost died. Our fleet began the Buggler Maneuver right away, and I authorized the discharge of Lucifer particles. It was an order to return fire. Then I thought, how did an attack from forty-seven light-seconds away get to us in less than 0.1 seconds? In outer space, distance was an absolute barrier. Nothing could bypass it.

The Proposal

The answer to my question was rather simple. The light containing the scene of the enemy fleet shooting a beam of light at us took forty-seven seconds to get to my eyes. And the Lucifer particles that were fired at that time also took forty-seven seconds to reach and fly past us. That was why the shooting and my observation of the shooting appeared to happen at the same time. The moment you realize that you are being shot at, you are shot without any time to prepare.

"Did you realize this, chief?" I asked the chief of staff, General Say More.

He answered, "Of course. You're the flagship operations officer, and you didn't think about this?"

Then he proceeded to give a long, elaborate explanation.

"Once upon a time, some nomads invaded a nation of settlers. Upon sighting the approaching nomads, the border patrol sent a messenger on the fastest horse they had to the capital to deliver the news. Several days later, the messenger arrived at the capital, but the next morning, the capital was already under siege by the enemy's vanguard. Because both the enemy's vanguard and the messenger rode their horses to the capital. As soon as the king received the message that the enemy crossed the border, the capital city was under attack. It's nothing new. As of now, the speed of light is the maximum speed limit for communication, and we reached that limit long ago, which means even as our civilization progresses, there are aspects that cannot but remain the same. The only thing left is for the speed of weapons to catch up to the speed of communication."

General Say More droned on for a while, but the entire time my heart was pounding. Because I'd witnessed the impenetrable, transparent wall of the universe being penetrated in an instant. It didn't matter that it was only an illusion. Because I had brushed with death. It was difficult to calm down. And it suddenly dawned on me. *We are really at war.* I'm grateful that they came all this way and found us—mere human beings whom they could've simply ignored—but the encounter certainly isn't as romantic as it sounds.

Taking the flagship's return fire as a signal, all our ships, which had been waiting for this moment, began to bombard the enemy fleet with Lucifer particles. As we had been in formation, ready for attack, our return fire was formidable. At minimum we must have tanked about a hundred of their ships.

The fight itself felt completely unrealistic. It would've been different had there been some sounds, but since there is no air in space, there is nothing but silence no matter how fierce the battle is. Without warning, devoid of tension, and unaware, you live or die. People are obliterated without the middle process. Like the ultimate, final judgment that is swiftly and summarily executed with no last defense, no struggle to escape death, and no shouting to the enemy, "Face the sword of justice!"

Until the hostilities ended, I stood, looking at the screen that displayed the battle site. Thousands and thousands of beams of light speeding toward or away from us. It reminded me of the time I watched the rain pour down on the streets of Seoul from the fiftieth floor. By your side.

I let out an exclamation without even realizing. Had I ever before seen a sight so beautiful? Cosmic rain streaks, flashing brilliantly every time they crossed the enormous wall of distance, as though determined to brighten the vast expanse of the entire universe. Friendly spaceships performing the Buggler Maneuver. The final flames of light that both enemy and friendly ships emit in the moment they are led by Lucifer particles into hell, spattering purgatory particles all around. I don't know if it's right to say that I really wish I could show you this scene. Perhaps it would be more moral to say that I wouldn't want such a sight to unfold in any other place in this universe. It was the most brutally beautiful sight. Like a gala of light-bearing demons.

5

To be honest, our accomplishments that day could hardly be called a victory, but General Liddell happily called it a great triumph. Probably because he wanted to report it that way to the UES Headquarters. Thanks to that, I received a new rank insignia ten days later, and there wasn't just one but two additional wings on it.

"I guess it's the price of my life," I said. "Had they been slightly more accurate with their shots, I would have been obliterated without a trace."

General De Nada remarked, "It's the price of the lives of those who died that day. It'll feel heavy for a while, your new insignia."

It was just as he said. Around that time, we heard the news that we would soon have reinforcements to replace those who were killed in action. There was a rumor about new ships as well, but that had been going around for years, so none of us put much stock in it. But, to our surprise, exactly one month after the battle, we heard that over two hundred new ships to replace the ones that had been destroyed had left the Earth's orbit. What was even more astonishing was that all of the new ships were assigned to the Inspection Force under the command of General Liddell.

General De Nada's expression didn't give anything away when the news reached him, but all the operations officers in the general staff knew which way General De Nada's heart had shifted. We all had a hunch that the hour of decision was near. When General De Nada puts his thoughts into action, should we follow him or not? Sure, this wasn't the first time that I had considered this, but because of my new insignia, the weight of my choice now felt heavier. And the hour of decision often comes sooner than expected.

One day, after I finished my shift and completed the transfer of duties, I stopped by the old cruiser and ran into General De Nada. At the exact place where the Rebel Force used to meet back in the day.

"Why don't you sit down for a minute," he said. "Don't worry, I won't mention the deployment plan for the next twenty-four hours. I'm on vacation until then, too. Come to think of it, being a commander isn't that great at times like this. It's not like someone's going to hand me a double

The Proposal

promotion, like the one you received. I have to get what I deserve myself."

I nodded as I approached him, and he pointed to a chair for me to sit down and said, "The bartender tells me that the Rebel Force hasn't gotten together in a while. Has it been disbanded? Or is it underground now? He says that you seem to have hit the ceiling of your leadership skills."

"Huh, I don't know about that. It's just that we have much better ways to spend our time these days, thanks to you, commander."

I was being sarcastic, of course. Silence followed. General De Nada wasn't much of a talker, and I didn't have much to talk about that day either. We simply sipped our drinks in silence for a while. It didn't matter that we didn't have much to say. We were there to take a break.

The old cruiser had been built without much consideration for artificial gravity. It was a cylindrical pillar with a protruding disk-like rim all around its middle, so when the ship spun, centrifugal force was created for the passengers to feel something like gravity. There was a room where you could play table tennis, but it wasn't very popular. Because the force of gravity created on that ship didn't act perpendicular to the surface. When you dropped a ball from the air, it fell at a slight angle in the direction of the ship's rotation, which always gave an advantage to one side of the table. It sort of sucked all fun out of the game, after a while.

The sleep room, though, was extremely popular because there were a lot of people who said they felt most comfortable when they slept with their backs flat "on the floor," even in space. But considering that they also wanted soft mattresses, I don't think they were talking about the actual floor as being comfortable.

The only reason people still frequented that old cruiser was that the cruiser was treated like a civilian area. There was no other reason to go there, really, since typical warships also had recreational facilities. I mean, our living quarters were all on the warships. And the facilities were pretty good too. But they weren't very popular for a single reason—they were classified as military facilities.

When the operation of the new cruiser was suspended due to the risk that it might expose the position of our fleet, the old cruiser became a popular destination once more. The visitors' area, in particular, was livelier than other areas thanks to people who were visiting from Earth. How can I describe it? It felt brighter and warmer. Above all else, you could see kids there. Crying, screaming, fighting, and running-without-looking children. That was the best kind of rest for me: spending time hovering around the visitors' area.

The Proposal

Everything looked different there. The soldiers looked like young men and women, and the older generals looked like elderly people. With a few children thrown into the mix, it was a perfectly ordinary scene. It made me feel like we were contributing to the ongoing creation of new generations. Like time would ultimately forgive us. I don't quite know what it is we did wrong. To need forgiveness, I mean.

I stared at General De Nada for some time. Even in the midst of such an ordinary scene, he seemed to be somewhat out of place, and it was hard to consider him an ordinary middle-aged man.

"So how come you're here, sir?" I asked. "You're not here to see someone, are you?"

His answer came about thirty seconds later. Even though he was literally sitting next to me. "Just people watching. Like a typical old man."

"I don't think you sitting there like that makes you a regular civilian. If you really wanted to feel that way, you should've gone to Earth. If this bar's owner is in his right mind, he couldn't possibly ask you to pay for that drink in your hand ... or mine, if I'm lucky."

General De Nada appeared somewhat tipsy already. I glanced next to him and noticed a palm-sized picture frame on the table before him. It was the one he kept in his office, containing a picture of his wife who died twenty years ago. So I asked, "Are you here to perform a memorial rite?"

He started and murmured, "You crazy Air Force bastards and the way you talk."

The general talked about his wife so much that everyone in the general staff knew her well. From how she was an intelligence officer of the Mars Orbit Force under the Allied Orbital Forces to how she completed her military service and returned to Earth. We'd heard his verbose explanations about how the human body had evolved to adapt to Earth's gravity, and thus staying too long in a place without gravity causes all the liquid in your body that should move downward end up staying too long in your upper body, making your face more swollen, and so the first time he met her in space, he wasn't particularly impressed about her appearance and only thought that she seemed to be a kind and generous person despite a long exposure to cutthroat competition. But then when he ran into her on Earth, he was surprised at how beautiful she was. We'd heard these stories so many times that we knew when to humor him and when to divert his attention. The picture in the frame was the image of his wife as she had been when the young commander met her by chance on Earth.

Gazing at the picture of his wife, General De Nada said,

The Proposal

"But I couldn't put my roots down on Earth. Even though my face looks somewhat swollen, this is our home, not Earth."

I scanned his face as he said those words. It certainly wasn't small. But then, he stared at me too. I felt as though it was now my turn to speak, so I said to him, "Wait, what is this? Did you just say that last bit to win me over to your side? Stirring solidarity between space-borns?"

He stood up and snorted, "Win you over my foot. What use would you be to me? They should teach you darned Air Force bastards to speak more politely. Anyway, I'll be going. Stay and have a few more drinks or go home." Then he pointed to the drink in my hand and said, "Ah, that drink is on me."

Did he need me, specifically? Or was he looking for anyone to support him? Whatever the case, all he gave me was one drink. One lousy drink.

In comparison, General Liddell offered me something much more valuable.

"Considering your capabilities, I can see you as a captain of a ship. Since we're at war, it's not like we would have to worry about promoting in order."

At his words, I took a deep breath and glanced around the room as though I was deep in thought. Trying to buy time.

General Liddell's office was much more refined and old-fashioned than I'd expected. The entirety of his flagship was full of classic and antique furniture. The Inspection Force's ships were the latest models with bodies wider than their lengths, and they also rotated at a faster speed compared to other ships, creating stronger artificial gravity. Added to that was the interior décor that gave the entire space a calm look, and as a result his office had a somber and imposing air.

The stronger artificial gravity had other effects too. It allowed for items from Earth to be placed here and there on the ship, since they could be held down in place with gravity. In his office, General Liddell had pieces of Earth furniture that were seldom seen in space fleets. I assume that each one had been strategically positioned to evoke the most solemn ambiance possible in the given space. But what made that room seem imposing was not the furnishing but the ceiling. The floor size of his office wasn't as big as I'd expected, but the height of the ceiling towered a distance greater than the combined length and width of the room.

"New ships will be deployed in combat soon. We have plenty of men in line to be promoted to captain, but I believe it's an opportunity to explore a fresh approach rather than adhering to the traditional process of promoting people in order."

There were three holy books sitting side by side on his

The Proposal

bookshelf. The first was the Bible featuring Jesus Christ—the belief of Earthians in the fundamental human feature of being able to distinguish between up and down. The next was *Prophecies*—the manifestation of the doubts that the land that humanity had been grounded in might not be as firm as we think; the prophecy of an the encounter with beings from somewhere beyond the universe, the ensuing war, and the culmination of these events being the emergence of an enigmatic celestial body known as the Temple of Doom, which would serve as a channel connecting this side of the universe to the world beyond; the declaration that the interdimensional portal would not only pour out extraterrestrial beings but gradually shift into Earth's orbit, eventually swallowing Earth whole and spitting it back out the other end. The holy book that stuck out, however, was the third one. It was the book that the UES was consulting in an effort to respond to all possible threats. Do you know what that book was? It was a guide on fleet tactics and strategies, penned by General De Nada.

"This is a model of the new ships," General Liddell spoke. "The Buggler Maneuver device has been built in. There are no better ships in terms of acceleration and fuel efficiency, and they have the greatest control range for regulating heat emissions. What do you think? You think you want one?"

I picked up the model of the new ship from his desk. I've checked the rules and found out that it's a violation for me to describe to you the exterior of the new ship in any documents that are sent outside the fleet. But it's not a problem to describe how the model was assembled. The thing about the model that caught my eye was not the shape of the model ship itself but a thin sliver of metal wire that was protruding on the bottom. I mean to say that the model ship was fixed on a base. To be placed on a desk in an office where gravitational forces were at work.

Had it been General De Nada's office, there'd be no need for such a base because you could simply float it in the air. It'd be easier to see the model that way, and it would more closely resemble the environment where the actual vessels would be deployed.

"This is the close-combat weapon system that we've recently ordered..."

While General Liddell explained to me the quality of the new weapons system, my mind wandered. I classified the possible errors that the Inspection Force would make into the categories of tactical and strategical, and I began to calculate which would be most detrimental to the entire fleet. This thought process all began because of that model ship. Because the model ship's base implied that they might

The Proposal

approach combat in space with the unnecessary premise of up and down. If that were to happen, there were bound to be blind spots in their tactics or strategies. There would be inevitable structural weak points that they wouldn't spot even if they were staring right at them.

I was curious about the new weapons system, but I was an operations officer, which meant that I would soon be hearing about it over and over and over again until I'm fed up. So I didn't think I needed to hear it right that second.

Finally, when he finished talking, General Liddell looked at me with a gratifying smile on his face. Only then I realized that it was time for me to respond to whatever it was that he had been explaining. But I had no idea what to say, since I hadn't listened to anything he'd said. The gist of his question was about deciding who to side with—him or General De Nada. It wasn't something that I was going to answer anyway. I wasn't the only one called to his office, a stream of people had already been called into that room before me, and we'd all agreed that it would be wise not to say anything at all. Until we received some kind of an order from above, it was safer not to take sides.

General Liddell waited a long time for my response, but eventually he gave in and spoke first.

"Well, give it some thought, then."

He meant that I could go and think about whatever it was on my own. I'd held out.

"Yes, sir!"

I saluted him, turned on my heels, and stepped out of his office. Right at that moment, a question struck me—had I ever saluted General De Nada upon leaving his office?

"You? Please. Never. Not even once. At this point, my expectations are low."

That was General De Nada's answer. I liked it. So I said, "I will salute you, sir, going forward."

The old man gazed at me for a long time, looking quite emotional. Then he said, "Why are you standing there like that? So what? You want me to be moved or something? Don't you know that you are supposed to salute me? Over there, see the *Crew Code of Conduct*? If you go and open it up, it will probably say that when you're leaving a superior's office, you must salute …"

It was going to be another long lecture. If I'd let him, he would've gone on like that for half an hour or even longer. So I pulled out a report on the next operational plan.

"Well, sir, about the next operational plan, what do you think about this? I just thought of this idea of using decoys to ambush the enemy ships …"

6

The decoys were camouflaged baits, devices that emitted radio signals equivalent to those of the fleet and thus potentially able to confuse the enemy regarding our actual positions. They weren't expensive, and I figured they would be useful for a number of things. When I looked into procuring them, though, it turned out that there were only a few manufacturers, which were all clustered around Earth's gravisphere, and so it would be difficult to get my hands on any. On top of that, at the time Earth was on the other side of the sun, the opposite of where we were stationed. The Allied Orbital Forces Command flatly said that they couldn't send us the decoys until a few months later, when Earth was closest to our fleet.

I mean, it wouldn't have cost that much to send them without delay. Considering the amount of money we normally wasted, it wouldn't have been a big deal. Had General Liddell requested the decoys to be sent over as soon as possible, they probably would have been. But our general staff was in an awkward position to be asking the Inspection Force for assistance. So we ultimately decided to relocate our fleet to a place that had been carpeted with decoys for billions of years.

"Since we can't get decoys to mimic us, we have no choice but to mimic the decoys," Chief of Staff Say More spoke with a look of resolute determination. A confident smile spread across his face.

And so we camped around the asteroid belt near Jupiter and behaved like we'd become asteroids, setting our course to travel in their orbit.

Navigation in outer space is a bit different from what Earth-borns think. All things in space move in one of three ways: one, revolve around a celestial body that has a gravitational force, like a planet; two, continue endlessly in a straight line in one direction; or three, stay in one place.

It's similar to the "celestial motion" that ancient people used to talk about. An absolutely perfect motion that differs from the imperfect motion on land. Although they can't move in perfect circles but rather ovals, celestial bodies must move in circular orbits. Whether it is a planet, a star, or God. That thought makes me rather somber. Imagine, mocking God's gait ...

We decided to destroy an asteroid and scatter the fragments.

The Proposal

On the rear side of Jupiter's orbital path, of the five spots where the gravitational pull of the Sun and Jupiter are nearly equal, we chose one of the two that were deemed relatively stable. Because asteroids were grouped together around there. Like the graves of sunken ships.

What we did was probably the largest-scale destruction of nature to ever have occurred outside of Earth. It wasn't an easy decision, but we didn't face many objections. Fragments of an asteroid, scattering across the universe in tens of thousands of directions. Although they were generally flowing in one path like a massive stream of water, following the original orbit of the asteroid, these countless meteoroids would eventually diverge, based on the impulse they received at the moment the asteroid exploded. Over time, a significant amount of meteoroids would be dispersed throughout the solar system, though most would likely fall toward Jupiter.

We rearranged the fleet in step with the speed and direction of the scattering meteoroids. We hid among them. Not behind the fragments, but rather we mingled with them. It wouldn't hide our location from the enemy forever, but it didn't matter as long as they couldn't pinpoint the exact positions of our ships.

Although we didn't know *how* they would come, we knew that the enemy would appear somewhere in our vicinity because they'd done it several times already. All we needed to do was to wait for them to show up. To seize that moment with the advantage on our side. What could be better than to conceal our positions? If they couldn't figure out our exact formation, they would have to choose one of two strategies— either spread out their assault ships to confirm our positions or form a close formation in one place to prevent being ambushed. We would first wait, and if the enemy ships seemed to be spread out, we would target the area where their ships were most thinly spread; if they seemed to be packed closely together, we would perform a turning movement and besiege them. Either way, they were bound to fail in preserving the optimal concentration of ships. The enemy would need to investigate first to understand the movements of the new meteoroids.

The problem was that this meant we also had to investigate and understand the movements of the new meteoroids, which meant we had a lot of work cut out for us. The entire general staff was busy establishing a formation plan for our ships in ambush zones, as well rearrangement plans in various scenarios in which our enemy would appear. We had to plan everything in advance. The plans were a headache that seemed to go on without end, but eventually they were completed. With Chief of Staff Say More borrowing two of the

The Proposal

latest astronomical observation ships from the Inspection Force Command, all our preparations were finished. Those ships were the finishing touches to our plans.

The ships were mounted with remarkable optical and radio telescopes. The telescopes were gigantic, and as an astronomy officer in the general staff remarked, it looked as though the ships were telescopes mounted with engines, rather than spacecrafts mounted with telescopes. The chief of staff temporarily assigned the telescopes to the Observation Bureau of the General Staff and summoned all astronomers in the fleet. I was also assigned to the Bureau.

"Okay, let's start our observations. We need to know everything, and I mean everything—don't miss a single thing."

A long silence ensued. We stopped the engines and began inertia navigation, mirroring the motion of the meteoroids around us and minimizing heat emissions from the ships, waiting for the enemy to appear. We were quietly, quietly sinking into the deep, pitch-black abyss that was the universe. Since there was no air for sound to travel though outside, we didn't hear anything. All I could hear was the sound of people next to me breathing. Even during the fiercest battles, with Lucifer particles slashing through the dark at the speed of light, outer space is always silent. Only the people on the spaceships make sounds, whether out of fear, surprise, or urgency.

I turned to the universe reflected in the telescopes. I heard that our fleet is full of astronomers who enlisted in the Allied Orbital Forces for the opportunity to work with those telescopes. They say that these telescopes are truly the best ones ever made by humanity. So why are they here instead of on Earth? To detect the presence of enemies. Because here, we're all distant as the stars to each other.

Long, long ago, in the ancient times, when nuclear weapons were first invented, someone proposed that we should launch a satellite into orbit and have it detect radiation on Earth, since it would allow them to check for traces of nuclear explosions on land. That would also help them see right away which countries were performing nuclear tests and the scale of the tests performed. The suggestion was accepted, and people ended up launching the satellite into space. The satellite went into operation and sent back the results of its first observation to the base on Earth. But the moment the people at the base saw the results, they were completely taken aback. Because signs of nuclear explosions were detected in too many places. It was chaotic, as though a nuclear war had already begun.

Eventually they learned that those signs had come from somewhere beyond the universe. There are ceaseless explosions occurring in space. Some were traces of explosions that occurred billions of years ago that finally arrived on Earth, while others were remnants of explosions from just hundreds of thousands of years ago. When you consider only the visible light areas, outer space seems steeped in darkness. But there are always exciting events taking place in the areas that are invisible to the human eye.

When you go into orbit and listen quietly, the universe reverberates with a cacophony of cheers so loud that mere nuclear explosions occurring in the distant corners of Earth's surface are nearly undetectable. So back then, there was only one way to differentiate those nuclear explosions on Earth—to map every signal that came from outer space. It meant detecting all the signals to gain a comprehensive understanding of all cosmic events, and then isolating the noises that couldn't be sorted into the categories of signals sent by the universe. Those remaining were the nuclear explosions humans created. So, humanity began to study the universe with money from the military. To figure out what their enemies were doing, different countries began to observe cosmic phenomena.

What we did was pretty much the same. Our fleet was lying in ambush amid the asteroid belt, surrounded by hundreds of thousands of meteoroids, and in order to detect the enemy fleet that came from somewhere beyond the universe to eliminate us, we had to know the movement of every single meteoroid. Sure, even the ancient Earthians had more than enough information on asteroids, but there was insufficient data on the fragments of the asteroid we'd destroyed—not to us nor to our enemy.

In other words, we had to understand everything about anything that could be seen from where the explosion took place—the entirety of outer space. That was why the fleet command and even the domineering Inspection Force Command didn't reprimand intelligence officers from the astronomical observation ships for using military telescopes to write academic articles in ordinary times. Because it was their job to know the minute details about the universe.

Those ships were astronomical observatories, moving in accordance with the rules of the celestial system on the quiet and desolate front line.

We remained in ambush for over five hundred hours. During that time, we first vented our frustrations about the incompetence of the UES Orbit Command, and then each of us delved into the character flaws of our direct supervisors in painstaking detail, and finally we classified the conspiracy theories on the identity of our enemy that were circulating in the fleet into largely five categories and evaluated the possibility of each theory. We were bored out of our minds.

The Proposal

Then, a little over 520 hours into our ambush operation, we received a report.

"Unidentified objects detected. Currently calculating the exact number. Moving at a speed similar to our ships. Now, accelerating."

We'd found a cluster of stars—stars of the enemy fleet.

That was how they always appeared. From the very first moment they were detected, they would be moving at about the same speed as our fleet, which could hardly be considered slow. And they would all be moving in more or less the same direction. In Earth terms, it was as if they didn't just fall from the sky but were actually racing at maximum speed the moment they appeared in the heavens.

How could they possibly have known our movements with such precision? Was there a spy among us? Or was our existence a direct factor that decided the manner of their emergence? However they managed to find us, they always did. And we were using that fact to our advantage in this ambush, but the more times I saw it happen, the stranger it seemed. Something always felt off about the way they appeared in our sights.

This fourth round of hostilities between us was the fiercest to date. From the expanse of the vast universe captured through the telescopes, we removed the detailed map that had been delineated by our astronomers, as though removing noise. Thousands of tiny but clear dots revealed themselves. As expected, the enemy fleet was approaching in a widely dispersed formation, coming toward the area where we were lying in ambush. That made sense since they had to figure out our formation.

As the general staff had planned in advance, General De Nada had our fleet in close formation. When the enemy ships came into the range of fire, we shot Lucifer particles in their direction. That signaled our entire fleet to prepare for combat. You know, performing the Buggler Maneuver and firing Lucifer particles.

The enemy ships began firing back, but because they were stretched so thin, only about half of their entire fleet participated in combat initially. It was exactly as we expected. Lucifer particles didn't get any less effective over distance, but the problem was the Buggler Paradox. As the distance increases, the effect of the Buggler Paradox intensifies, and beyond a certain distance, the accuracy rate of the shots drops to almost zero. It virtually creates an effective firing range, which means that ships that are too far away become useless.

Momentarily, we had a numerical advantage. Since we were neck and neck with the enemy in terms of artillery accuracy rate, we had a clear advantage in this situation.

The Proposal

Streaks of light rained down. Lucifer particles flashed with terrifying brilliance throughout the battlefield. Some flew toward us, while others dashed toward enemy ships. Of course, we couldn't see everything with the naked eye, but we had two astronomical telescopes. If not for them, it would've taken us much longer to figure out what was going on, since we would have had to use images captured by telescopes positioned around Earth. But this time we used the telescopes to assess the situation within minutes.

In previous combats, those few minutes were critical. In a bad way for us, because the enemy ships used to appear out of the blue. They didn't approach us like a comet, gradually nearing us from afar so that we could tell which way they were coming. Rather, they would appear out of nowhere, as if jumping out of some underground tunnel, and ambush us. Every time, our positions were fully exposed to the enemy.

But now, the tables had turned. Having high-performance telescopes nearby was quite significant in terms of tactics as well. The effects became apparent right away. After the combat began, we received the following report:

"The enemy ships in combat are attempting to escape. Accelerating in reverse now. Leaving the orbit."

"Orbit" referred to the orbital path of the original asteroid, which hundreds of thousands of big and small meteoroids that were acting as our decoys, as well as our ships and the enemy ships, were all following. If you think of the orbit as a current, the enemy fleet was chasing us from behind along the current, before they began reversing.

Then, General Liddell's Inspection Force began to accelerate in reverse as well, chasing after the retreating enemy ships. The rest of our fleet was waiting for an order from General De Nada.

"Should we go after them?"

"Wait," the general said.

General De Nada appeared to be watching the enemy ships rearrange their formation. The rest of us were also keeping an eye on them. It was clear that the enemy's changed formation wasn't that of a fleet fleeing from a fight. Through our telescopes, we saw the enemy fleet transition into a defensive position with finesse while maintaining a close formation and leaving the battlefront. With a defensive line like that in place, there was no point in pursuing them. Because they weren't fleeing in defeat. After a short time, General De Nada ordered the entire fleet to stop chasing the enemy, but the Inspection Force continued after the enemy ships on their own for a while. Of course, eventually General Liddell had to give up the chase as well.

That was when it happened. Our eyes darted to the screens

The Proposal

showing the images captured by the telescopes. Because right at that moment, the retreating enemy fleet suddenly vanished from our view. We couldn't detect them at all, not with optical telescopes or radio telescopes.

"What just happened?" Chief of Staff Say More asked, but I didn't really have an answer for him.

"What happened?" General De Nada asked. "Have they been wiped out?"

That was impossible, of course. Even if some accident occurred and destroyed the entire fleet, there were bound to be debris and fragments.

"What the heck … what on Earth are they?"

Someone murmured quietly, and that was exactly my thought. Where in the world did they come from and where did they disappear to? When they weren't here attacking us, where were they and what were they doing? What we'd witnessed contained a clue to these questions that we've had for decades—it turned out, they weren't hiding somewhere undetected, preparing for the next attack; rather, they had vanished into the depths of the universe.

"That's a clue?" The chief of staff asked me when I voiced my thoughts. "So where do they disappear to?"

But he probably knew the answer himself because it had crossed all our minds. What it said in *Prophecies*. The interdimensional portal that connected Earth to somewhere beyond the universe. It was there, not too far from us, in a place that was much closer to us than we thought. The mysterious celestial body called the Temple of Doom.

That made me wonder, who were we fighting anyway? Is that fleet really our enemy? Or were we fighting with something even greater? Man, what the hell are we doing?

It was a strange war. But why hadn't I thought about these points more seriously before?

Suddenly, I was overcome with a sense of betrayal. What the enemy fleet was doing felt like a betrayal. They hadn't come to us fair and square, by crossing the enormous wall of distance. I mean, it made sense. If they had, it would've taken them millions of years, or even longer, who knows? They must have used a shortcut. The Prophet hinted as much, and even without his prophecies all of us guessed as much. That there was a shortcut somewhere. One of the reasons we had camped out in the asteroid belt was to prove that—and to test the capabilities of the interdimensional portal.

Yet, the moment I witnessed the existence of that passage, I couldn't help but think that our enemy—the sole force capable of challenging our fleet, the adversary I had thought we were fighting fair and square—had actually been playing foul. We'd been working like dogs to fight them, operating under

The Proposal

the genuine belief that outer space required us to proceed step by step and overcome every hurdle with integrity.

A sense of futility washed over me.

7

It was around this time that you came to visit. The time I began to question the meaning of my work.

"Aren't you happy to see me?" you asked.

"I'm happy to see you," I answered.

Your face had gotten big like the faces of people living here. And perhaps that was why your smile seemed foreign to me.

"I heard that the new cruiser you told me about isn't operational now. I came to see how great it was, but when I asked about it, they told me that you were probably the one who put it out of use."

Why did you feel so unfamiliar? Why did our rendezvous feel so awkward? Was it because we had been out of touch for a while? Or was it because I had too many things on my mind?

"Oh, I suppose that's somewhat true. Technically, they're not wrong. It was the general staff that issued the order, and I am a general staff member."

"What? I've been cheated! I came all the way here because I heard about how great the new cruiser was from you."

Came all the way. That was what you said. From Earth to here, you crossed the vast expanse of outer space to visit me. Not by boring a hole somewhere in the wall of distance, but by traveling meter by meter, or kilometer by kilometer, honestly and gradually closing the distance between us.

"Sorry I haven't been in touch more frequently," you said. "I didn't tell you because you never asked, but I …"

But how were the enemy ships appearing as soon as they left the interdimensional portal? The memory of the last battle kept on popping into my head. In particular, the enemy fleet's formation immediately after our telescopes detected them.

"It's fine," I answered. "Don't worry about it. I didn't write you as often either because of the operation."

"But still."

They had no idea what formation we were in as we were lying in ambush. They knew nothing about what we were doing. Yet I hadn't sensed any hesitance on their part. They were taking confident strides toward something. As if they knew exactly where their target was. How? How was that possible? I tried to recall what happened. The direction they were headed to that day! All of a sudden, a strange feeling came over me. A hunch of an operations officer of the general staff,

The Proposal

perhaps? It was something that I'd felt in battle that day, a fleeting thought that had come to me before vanishing just as fast. Now it filled my head once more. I'd known it that day. I knew exactly where the enemy fleet had targeted.

"I'm sorry," you said.

I answered, "It was the flagship!"

"Flagship? Did you hear anything I said?"

"Huh?"

Their target was the flagship. It was as if they knew the exact position of the flagship from the start. They were after General De Nada.

"Are you listening to me?"

The news of your visit spread across the general staff. Which was a problem because the members of the general staff were spread out across the entire fleet.

"I heard you broke up with her," Chief of Staff Say More said out of the blue. "What happened? She came all the way here, and you just turned her away?"

"Who said I turned her away? How much has the rumor snowballed? We're still together. I'm going to see her after work. If you're so worried about my relationship, maybe you should let me get off work early."

But at that time, the general staff couldn't afford to let

people who'd come to work go home early. In fact, they often had to bring those who had gone home to sleep back in to work. The biggest task at hand was to figure out the whereabouts of the vanished enemy fleet, and the next was to study and analyze the enemy fleet's response maneuver to our ambush. I volunteered for the former, but General De Nada reassigned me to the analysis team, and so I couldn't dig further into what I wanted to learn.

General De Nada appeared to be shocked by the enemy fleet's movement during our previous combat. Actually, "impressed" might be a better word. We couldn't move so fluidly yet. Spaceships are no airplanes and are dominated by an enormous inertia, which makes it difficult for each spaceship to change direction at will or come to a stop at once. Essentially, they're like sailboats, being swept away in the rapids. No matter what formation the command demands, it's not easy to move the spaceships into the intended positions. Every ship needs to be manned by an experienced pilot for the entire fleet to change formation as necessary. And the enemy fleet was doing that without difficulty. It meant that there was a huge gap between our training exercises and combat experiences.

"Looks like the general wants us to be like them, right?" said Chief of Staff Say More.

"He wants us to do that? That's almost an aerial show. To

The Proposal

do that kind of a maneuver, we would have to have ships with far superior capabilities. But all the best ships belong to the Inspection Force, so unless we siphon off some of those ships, how else could we possibly pull that off?"

"More training?"

"I don't know. Would we really be able to do that with more training?"

Rumors of intensifying maneuver training were already rampant in the fleet. General De Nada wasn't the only one who sensed the deficit in our navigation skills; it was conspicuous enough for all of us to notice.

"With extra training, we might really end up feeling like we're in the Marines. But in any event, where do we start? We'd need an analysis of the L-22 beam's accuracy rate, an analysis of the enemy fleet's Buggler Maneuver pattern during their retreat, a plan to simplify the dissemination of the fleet rearrangement order in an emergency …"

"I'll take the accuracy rate analysis," I answered, gathering all relevant sources and heading to the astronomical observation ship mounted with a radio telescope. Nowhere else provided a better environment for tracking purgatory particles. The analysis involved using the detected purgatory particles to trace the trajectories of Lucifer particles. We couldn't possibly track all of the Lucifer particles, so my task was to look through the statistics on shots fired by each echelon and focus on the ones that stood out. At first glance, certain results caught my eye. They were statistics on gunfire from the flotilla where P, a colleague in the general staff, was attached. Their accuracy rate was significantly lower compared to others in the fleet. I contacted P and asked him about it.

"Why is your accuracy rate hitting the bottom?" I asked. "Was it some kind of mechanical failure?"

"I don't know. I would think mechanical failure if it were one ship, but it doesn't make sense for all ten ships of the flotilla to be affected."

"Perhaps it's you. There's no other common factor, you know."

"Oh, you're just asking to get your ass kicked, aren't you."

I pulled up the combat data recorded by the telescope and requested the Observation Bureau backtrack the purgatory particles detected in the frontal area of P's flotilla. A while later, the Bureau sent me the data showing the trajectories of Lucifer particles.

That was when an observation officer said to me, "We're not at a point where we can tell you this with certainty, and we would have to investigate further before we can give you a concrete conclusion, but it wasn't an error on the gunners' part. It seems like there was something there."

The Proposal

"What do you mean?"

"Like I said, we're not sure yet, but the distance calculation was off for the aims. There was a slight distortion in that area in the astronomical observation data distributed by the Observation Bureau. Since the locations of the enemy ships were calculated based on that data, the distance was thrown off."

"Is it the Bureau's mistake?" I asked.

"We are investigating with that in mind, but it doesn't look that way."

"Then what is it?"

"It's no one's fault. There was something there on the enemy fleet's rear side."

"Huh?"

"You don't see anything, right?" the observation officer asked. "The telescopes didn't capture anything there, but there was something there."

"How do you know that if the telescopes couldn't record it?"

"We compared the images taken during combat to ones taken prior, and behind the target enemy ships, there was a fixed star that we used as a reference to calculate the enemy position. It became slightly brighter during the combat."

"It got slightly brighter? What does that mean?"

"We have to study it more and see if the change in the star's brilliance is significant. If it is correct that the star brightened momentarily during combat, we have to consider this—since the star was a stable one, it's not likely that the light source itself brightened suddenly. Instead, it would make more sense to say that it temporarily appeared brighter to our eyes. It means that the rays of light that would have spread out more widely under normal circumstances were marginally refracted to our direction and converged."

I was surprised. "That means, it sounds like you're saying ... Are you saying that there was a gravity lens behind the enemy fleet?"

"Yes, that is what we suspect."

"That means ..."

"Exactly what you are thinking."

It meant that space was warped. A bed sheet is a two-dimensional plane on a bed, but when someone sits down on the sheet, the part where the person is sitting sinks under their weight. Were you to roll a ball around that area of the bed where the person is sitting, its path would be warped toward the sunken section. If you marked the ball's trajectory on the bed sheet and placed the bed sheet on a flat surface again, it would appear as if the ball had traveled in an arc for no reason. As though someone had pulled on it. An object

The Proposal

with mass bends the space around it. Even rays of light bend when passing through that space. Not because someone's pulling them, but because the space itself is shaped that way.

That was what the observation officer was saying. That the space on the rear side of the enemy fleet was slightly distorted, and as a result the light from the star that passed through it was brighter, as if it had passed through a magnifying glass. It meant that there was an invisible object with a rather large mass between the enemy fleet and the star.

"What could it possibly be?" I asked. "Are you saying that there was a gate to an interdimensional portal there?"

"Could be."

Could it really have been an interdimensional portal? At that stage, even the Observation Bureau couldn't have confirmed what it was. Since most of the people who work at the Bureau are scientists, they wouldn't have said much until they saw some proof for themselves. But there was one indisputable fact—the enemy fleet that was traveling in that direction suddenly vanished.

"Let me know as soon as you get the results."

"Sure, of course."

After our conversation, I flew over to Chief of Staff Say More and explained to him what my task should be in future combat.

He asked, "Are you sure?"

"No," I replied.

"If you're not even sure, do you think the higher ups will approve the operational plan?"

Some time later, I received news that the operational plan was approved, along with a directive to design a more detailed scheme.

That was what happened. After all that, I went back to the hotel in the old cruiser where you had been staying, but you were already gone. I felt as though there were still traces of your warmth left in the room, but it must have been my imagination. I stood in the center of the room and quietly listened. I didn't hear any sound. No music, no creaking doors, no retreating footsteps. When I turned toward the hallway, I noticed the note you'd left on the inside of the door.

I don't think it's time for us to be together yet. I'll be waiting for you. Come find me when it's time.

I stared at your note in silence. Okay. When it's time.

8

The fifth combat wasn't a fight for victory. It was more like an observational experiment. While our fleet exchanged fire with the enemy, I mobilized all astronomical observatory ships mounted with radio telescopes, arranging them on the outskirts of the battlefield to comb over the enemy fleet's rear to check whether a new gravity lens had formed. When you have a number of radio telescopes arranged that way, they work together as though you have a single, gigantic radio telescope big enough to cover the entire battlefield. It allows you to see even smaller spots in more detail.

The problem was that the observation ships couldn't perform the Buggler Maneuver. If the ships mounted with telescopes moved chaotically instead of following prearranged routes, it'd be impossible to use the radio signals reflected by each telescope to restore an image as a whole. To get an image, the ships had to move in an agreed-upon pattern. A relatively simple pattern at that. It meant that the moment the pattern of our movements was exposed to the enemy, we could lose all of the observation ships in our fleet. That was why General De Nada allowed me only a short time for my plan.

Just as we'd expected, soon after the shooting started, the enemy fleet began to concentrate their artillery fire on the observation ships. They'd noticed the pattern.

"You have four minutes starting now," the general said to me. "Figure it out within that time and clear the pattern. I can't give you more time. If we lose all those observation ships, it'll be like fighting with our eyes shut."

At that moment, our observational equipment picked up a gravity lens.

"We found one. Transmitting the location data now."

Chief of Staff Say More, who was on General De Nada's flagship, took the information I sent him and disseminated it throughout the entire fleet. Then all the vessels in our fleet stopped firing and directed their weapons toward where the gravity lens had emerged. Just as we had planned in advanced.

"Weapons at the ready. Commence firing in oh-five-four seconds. Open fire!"

After General De Nada issued the command—which was timed exactly as General De Nada had planned—all assault ships in our fleet began to fire Lucifer particles toward the gravity lens. Immediately afterward came another directive.

"Cease fire for seven-oh seconds!"

After the massive beam of light flashed across the battlefield, we ceased firing and responded to the enemy's attacks only with the Buggler Maneuver. It felt as though the previously tumultuous battlefield suddenly fell silent. The previous sporadic rays of light carrying Lucifer particles were nothing compared to the great flash of light we'd just created.

It was true that the enemy ships' sporadic yet aimed shots posed a much greater threat than our flashy volley fire. No matter how intense, a volley couldn't possibly inflict much damage to an enemy fleet when there was only one ship in an area the size of Earth. Our target, however, wasn't an enemy vessel. In fact, our volley fire didn't intend to hit anything. It was to see how that particular area was warped. During the seventy seconds of lull, our observation ships recorded every detail of the battlefield, capturing images of where the Lucifer particles passed up to a distance of seventy light-seconds.

"Compiling completed."

Finally, the Observation Bureau informed us they had finished, and simultaneously the observation ships began the Buggler Maneuver while our assault ships resumed shooting at the enemy fleet. The hostilities continued until the enemy fleet vanished without a trace once again.

When the combat ended, a strange sense of relief came over me. Like sleep that I had been holding off for a long time.

We decided on a location to set up camp and summoned all repair equipment, cruisers, and other rear facilities to that area. When I laid eyes on the old cruiser where you had been staying, a corner of my heart felt hollow. I stopped by the cruiser after work, and it looked as though the place where you had once sat was slightly distorted. Your gravitational field was still there—a gravitational field that didn't affect anyone else and was only visible to me.

You might not understand. You might even say that such things don't exist. But here in this fleet, I have seen countless, uncrossable barriers between Earth-borns and space-borns like myself. Differences that seem so trivial and thus more fundamental, inherent to our lives. These are things that slip out without thinking, things that, every time there is a conflict, make you feel as though the other person is encroaching on the most essential part of you. It seems that I'm not the only one who feels this way because my space-born colleagues who are dating someone on Earth talk about these same difficulties. When my colleagues and I get together and talk about such predicaments, I start to wonder that maybe we'd become a different species from Earth-borns.

The Proposal

But I think those are all untruths. I hope they are. You know what I end up thinking? I don't hate the gravity field you left behind. The moment I trace the huge void left behind in the place where you once stayed and rekindle your presence in my heart—the moment I revive the silhouette of your existence once again—I realize how much I've been longing, yearning for everything to return to the way it was!

Unfortunately, not everyone shared my thoughts. The next day, I was summoned by General Liddell to the Inspection Force Command. He asked me if I'd found out anything. I told him that I hadn't yet received the detailed analysis results, but that we seemed to have found what we were looking for. Then the old man told me that he also seemed to have found something. I couldn't help but be concerned about what it was that he was going to nitpick at this time.

"What is it that you found, sir?" I asked him.

"Well, let's talk about what you found first, the Temple of Doom."

"We can't say that for certain yet, sir."

"Sure. But whatever it is, it's true that the enemy fleet comes through it and then vanishes into it again. Am I right?"

"Yes, sir."

"What are your thoughts?" General Liddell asked. "What

do you think is beyond that portal? What I'm asking is, where do you think they're coming from? Somewhere beyond the universe?"

"Well, sir, that's not really my area of expertise. The UES Headquarters should …"

A moment of silence followed. Which General Liddell then broke.

"I'm asking you to speculate."

"Why does my speculation matter?"

"It matters."

"I don't follow, sir."

General Liddell responded slowly, "We need to be prepared."

"For what, sir?"

"Mutiny."

I was speechless for a moment. Mutiny, again? I tried to keep my voice calm, but it was much more difficult than I thought.

"Are you saying that there are rebel forces beyond the portal, sir? I am not sure what you are thinking, sir, but whatever it is, it can't be rebel forces."

"Just listen to me."

"If they are already there, sir, how can they be the rebel forces? Aren't the rebels that the Inspection Force are afraid

The Proposal

of anchored right over there? And the key person is probably in the Fleet Commander's Office right about now."

"I know what you're trying to say," said General Liddell. "And we haven't tried to hide who we have been after. Everyone knows that the Inspection Force has an eye on General De Nada. And I understand what you will think now that I've said what I said. You think that the Inspection Force is making up delusional charges to eliminate General De Nada. Am I right?"

"Something like that, sir."

"You're right. General De Nada himself hasn't done anything. Yet. But if you look at the evidence we uncovered, you wouldn't think it a delusion. Because it's nearly confirmed."

"Then show me, sir."

"Certainly."

General Liddell waved his hand and a three-dimensional screen popped up over his desk. It was a familiar scene. Seeing as how the asteroid fragments were floating around, it seemed like a replay of the fifth combat. I stared at the screen as if to bore a hole in it.

"You know what this is, don't you?" he asked.

"Of course, sir."

He then touched the screen to zoom in on one specific point. He kept on zooming in until it was impossible to see what was happening in combat and finally stopped. He had zoomed in on an enemy ship, which was shown on the screen.

General Liddell asked, "Do you know what this is?"

"You've zoomed into the enemy camp, so I assume it's an enemy ship."

"That is correct. Have you seen it before?"

"This is the first time I'm seeing this particular kind, sir."

"Makes sense. It's the only one of its kind in their fleet."

"Is it the flagship, sir?"

"Perhaps. It might be a ship designed for a particular purpose, but we are almost certain that it is the flagship."

"I see."

At my answer, General Liddell said, "I thought you'd be curious. As to how we became certain that it is the flagship."

"I didn't think you were going to tell me, sir. How did you come to that conclusion?"

General Liddell paused for a second before he continued. "When you're in the Allied Orbital Forces Headquarters, you get to witness a lot of interesting things. Particularly in unexpected places, where you would never expect to see anything interesting. For instance, when they open submissions for new ship designs, there are companies that submit existing designs. What is troubling about this is that their designs are often that of enemy ships, rather than our own. It leaves those

The Proposal

in charge of selecting ship designs dumbfounded. Wouldn't you be? What would you do, if you were in charge? As someone in the field general staff?"

Rather than wait for my answer, he went on. "What we do on Earth is, we first eliminate the design from the list of candidates and then conduct a background check on the company. To figure out how they obtained that design, down to the most intricate details. It's reasonable to suspect that they're in league with the enemy. So we start investigations, but even while doing so some things still remain a mystery. For instance, why submit such a design in the first place? Isn't that strange? Let's say that you somehow got your hands on such information. Why would you hand it back over to us? Trying to mock us or something?"

"I suppose it would be to show off," I answered. "To prove they have the capability to acquire such information."

"Yes, I'd much prefer that to be the reason. But the strange thing is, there's nothing special about these companies when you actually dig into them. In most cases, they have no connection to combat fields. Nor do they look as though they would have a lot to gain by showing off their intelligence skills. Nevertheless, it keeps on happening. Whenever we're about to move on, it happens again. Then recently, we found the most unusual thing."

General Liddell pointed to the enemy ship still hovering on the screen above his desk. "This is it. This is the first time we've seen this ship. I don't know whether this was just the first time we found it or whether this combat was the first time this ship was deployed. Whatever the case, we had no observational records of this ship."

"So what, sir?"

"So what? Well, the Allied Orbital Forces' Logistics Command recently sent us the blueprint of a new ship that was to be introduced to the fleet. Coincidentally, that ship looks like this."

General Liddell stretched out his hand in front of him, and another three-dimensional screen appeared from the ceiling. The screen displayed a 3D blueprint of the new ship.

"What do you think? What do you think when you look at these two?"

The moment I laid my eyes on the two screens, I was at a loss for words. Because it was, undoubtedly, the same ship. They looked identical, so much so that someone who didn't know anything about them would have thought that one was a blueprint, and the other was a completed model.

Without a word, General Liddell looked at me for a long time, as I stood speechless, racking my brain to come up with something to break the silence.

The Proposal

"So, the Inspection Force thinks—" I began to speak, but General Liddell cut me off.

"You wouldn't know it here, but this shook up the Allied Orbital Forces' Logistics Command. Around that time, a new hypothesis was floated, which is relevant to my earlier question to you. The thing that you discovered. The unidentified celestial object called the Temple of Doom or whatnot. What do you think is there, beyond that portal?"

"*Prophecies* says that it's another dimension, sir. The other side of the universe."

"It does. That's what we've believed so far. I'm not asking you because I didn't know that. In my time, we had to memorize *Prophecies*. The new theory that's been floating around the UES these days is that what is on the other side of the portal isn't the other side of the universe."

"Then what …?"

"The other side of time," General Liddell answered. "In other words, they're saying that the enemy fleet didn't come from another spatial dimension but from another time. This may also sound delusional to you, but when you think about it, things fit. Take the Lucifer particle guns, for instance. The oddest thing is, how did the enemy fleet that came all the way across the universe come to arm themselves with the exact same weapons as we did? I'm not so sure about Lucifer particles indeed being the most typical weapons in space. Don't you agree?"

Only then I realized what it was that he was trying to say. It was what he talked about all the time—who are rebels, and at the same time, who is the enemy fleet.

"It's obvious that De Nada will start a mutiny," said General Liddell with a look of resolute determination.

"That doesn't make sense, sir."

"Doesn't it? I think it does. This new ship you see here was going to be introduced to the fleet five years from now. Under the assumption that the war will continue until then. Each development stage is set to commence only with the confirmation that the war is ongoing, so it's very much possible that the ship might not be introduced to the fleet in the next ten years. Yet that ship is here, now, in the enemy camp. Take a look over here. Have you seen this image before?"

General Liddell was pointing at a coat of arms. I'd never seen it before, but I could guess whose it was.

"This is De Nada's coat of arms. One thing is for certain— ironically, the enemy that we are fighting against is none other than ourselves. We've come this far, expending tremendous amounts of resources, only to find out that we've been swinging our fists at our reflection in the mirror. I don't know what this means. As you've said, it might not be my

The Proposal

area of expertise. My task is something else entirely. It's about preventing further sacrifices. There is a solution. I just don't feel confident enough yet. The suspect hasn't taken any action either, so I have no grounds for punishment, at least as of now."

"Why are you telling me all this, sir?"

"You're not the only one who's hearing about this. I aim to announce it to the entire fleet soon. When that happens, things are going to get rather chaotic, so I'm telling a few people in advance. That's about all you need to know."

"My question is, sir, what is the reason for letting me know in advance?"

"Can't you see? I am telling you to not join the rebels. Never. Because you're someone who deserves to know this in advance."

"It still sounds delusional to me, sir. Doesn't it sound too much like a dream?"

"Does it? Well, it doesn't matter. If this is something that the entire Allied Orbital Forces is dreaming, then soon it will come true."

As General Liddell had told me, the rumor spread like wildfire through the fleet—the rumor about how someone would soon start a mutiny and that our enemy seemed to know who it was. Then chaos ensued. The whole fleet was agitated. Only General De Nada didn't seem to be disturbed. In a word, it was delusional, he seemed to imply.

"Looks like they will stop at nothing to get what they want," said Chief of Staff General Say More. That was the overall opinion of the general staff because there were too many holes in the UES's theory. In fact, the theory never even became the Allied Orbital Forces' official position. Nevertheless, the Inspection Force seemed to act ever more certain. Things worsened, as new ships were once again assigned to the Inspection Force, which meant that over half of the right to command was handed over to the Inspection Force Command. It was like there were two fleets under the Allied Orbital Forces. Yet, General De Nada didn't seem the least affected.

"It's nice to have two fleets," he said nonchalantly. "And fleets should exist in the plural. In which country do they assign all the military force under the command of a single person? No one can effectively lead such a huge group anyway."

"But we are run as a de facto single unit. And we have a single task. There is no point in dividing the entire fleet into two, but they're forcing it, and that's what gets to me."

"Well, say we're just two allied fleets."

"Shouldn't you be doing something, sir?"

"Like what? Are you telling me that I should start a mutiny for real? If I let the rumor bother me, it does nothing other than making the old man Liddell a real prophet. Clearly,

The Proposal

having that many stars on his uniform isn't enough, so now he's trying to be an oracle. Let's just move onto another topic—your observational report. Where is it? When are you going to pay for the seven observation ships you blew up?"

I was obliged to pull up the analysis data of the L-22 beam trajectories compiled by the Observation Bureau. The paths made by Lucifer particles were marked in pale blue light, which suddenly illuminated the dark interior of the office. There were more than 1,700 lines in the air. As General De Nada looked over the screen, his face also displayed a stark contrast of light and darkness.

The fighting had taken place across a rather vast area. To have as many ships as possible participate in the combat, the basic strategy was to arrange our formation in a wide, hemispherical shape, as if attempting to encircle the enemy. And since the enemy fleet did the same, there were two huge hemispheres in the battlefield. Where the flat bases of the hemispheres faced each other was the frontline. The image I pulled up in the commander's office displayed the trajectories of the Lucifer particles fired by our L-22 artillery up to the distance of seventy light-seconds all towards a single point, and as a result, the shape of our fleet on the screen was closer to an ice cream cone, rather than a hemisphere.

General De Nada knew exactly which point was the important one in the image. He approached the area behind the enemy fleet where Lucifer particles converged into a sharp point and examined it.

"Is this it?" he asked.

"Yes, sir. The location is marked. It is about 62.7 light-seconds from our fleet, and the Lucifer particle paths were all distorted at that point. It is, of course, difficult to confirm with the naked eye ..."

Past the enemy fleet, about 62.7 light-seconds from our own fleet, a minute but clear gravity lens phenomenon was captured by our telescopes. And the Temple of Doom must have been at the center of it. Although I'd told General Liddell that I couldn't be certain, there was really no other possibility. It was nothing other than the Temple of Doom mentioned in *Prophecies*.

"How much mass does it have?" General De Nada asked.

"According to the Observation Bureau, enough to create an orbital interference in the asteroid belt. I think they suspect that it might have caused a perturbation of Jupiter."

With a look of curiosity, General De Nada examined the spot where Lucifer particles converged. He slowly stretched out his hand to touch that point, and for some strange reason he looked so forlorn. His eyes were on one thing only,

The Proposal

as though his soul had been taken away, as though he were gradually being sucked into it. That's right. He knew it. He knew that the enemy was targeting him. That as soon as the enemy ships came through the Temple of Doom, they were headed toward him.

"Are there traces of movement?" General De Nada asked. "Did this move by itself?"

"Yes, sir. Its speed is about the same as the average speed of our fleet prior to initiating combat. The presumption is that the enemy fleet was able to keep up with us in our inertial orbit because the gateway itself had movements that were nearly identical to ours."

It must have been that exact feeling. The feeling that I got every time General Liddell summoned me to his office. The awareness that, surprisingly, I was an important person to some people. General De Nada must have thought the same thing, seeing the mysterious visitors who came through the interdimensional portal keep coming for him instead of heading to Earth—*To them, I'm more of a threat than the Allied Orbital Forces Command.*

Ultimately, the Inspection Force must have been thinking the same—that General De Nada was a threat. That strange suspicion that General De Nada was the leader of a rebellion that hadn't even been fomented yet? That was probably fate.

9

A few days before the sixth combat began, I stopped by the sea and ordered a ring. There's a new zero-gravity jewelry shop that opened there.

Did I tell you that we now have a sea here? It's more like an aquafarm, but we call it the sea. It's a gigantic saltwater aquarium for farming space species of fish and shellfish that are able to reproduce in zero gravity. I stop by every now and then to watch them. When I see them swimming in the zero-gravity sea, where there is no "up" or "down," it feels like they might have an operations officer of the general staff among them. Because there are times when the school of fish moves as one just like a fleet. Despite the fact they are unable to stay facing the same direction, each fish looking a different way, with their backs facing whichever way they perceive as up.

Most Earth species of fish can't adapt to a zero-gravity sea.

They lose all sense of balance and feel as though they are constantly falling. So, they keep swimming "upward." On their part, they're swimming as best they can to stop falling. But no matter how much they try, the feeling of falling doesn't subside. Because wherever they end up swimming to isn't "up," and they swim upward again, this time to a new "up." They end up swimming round and round, drawing a big circle with the back of their heads.

I wonder if the perfect circular movements that gods of the celestial world used to perform were something like that. That is, whether divine providence has also been imprinted in the hearts of fish. It seems as though Earth species of fish can't even dream that it doesn't matter which direction they are facing because all directions are the same. They believe that there is a clearly defined "right" state of balance and that they must continue flipping themselves over to find it. But in that zero-gravity sea, water doesn't flow from top to bottom. It remains together because of tension.

But there are a few species that have evolved from Earth fish species and have adapted well to zero-gravity seas. Even though they all swim in the same direction, their backs face different directions. That's me. A fish who doesn't understand divine providence. A fish who believes that I am in the "right" state of balance, regardless of which way I'm facing. General

The Proposal

De Nada's one of them too, as are thousands of space-born crew members who follow him.

"You ordered a ring I heard," said General De Nada. "For your girlfriend?"

The news that I visited the jewelry shop seemed to have spread throughout the entire general staff. I said yes. He was deep in thought for a while, and then he told me to get off the flagship and move to an escort vessel.

"Is this a demotion? Because I ordered a ring?"

"You're the only one who cares about the ring. Get a grip. Haven't you noticed them? It feels like they're boring a hole into the back of my head. Do something about them."

He was talking about the school of Inspection Force fish, who still believed that they were falling but now seemed to have bottled up the urge to keep on spinning backward and had our entire fleet surrounded from all sides. They were squeezed up next to us within a distance where the Buggler Paradox didn't manifest, so they could attack us at any moment. It was much too obvious. And insulting enough to make even the most loyal person want to start a mutiny. That must have been General Liddell's intention—provocation.

However, General De Nada still didn't seem too bothered. But even from a purely operational perspective, facing the enemy fleet while being surrounded by the Inspection Force was the same thing as completely giving up the right to command. The Allied Orbital Forces treated us like a group of foreign mercenaries. Through the chief of staff, I opined to General De Nada that it would be best to abandon our participation in combat, but of course General De Nada did not accept my suggestion. The chief of staff relayed me the general's answer and said, "I'm sure he has something in mind. Trust him on this."

But no matter how much I thought about it, I couldn't think of a plan.

"It's not a matter of trust, sir. It's like entering a battle while carrying your mother-in-law on your back. Those Inspection Force bastards, it doesn't look like they're going into combat with the enemy. More like they'll be targeting us."

The only thing that had improved compared to the previous battle was the three thousand new decoys we received thanks to our mother-in-law, a.k.a. the Inspection Force, contacting the Allied Orbital Forces Command. Those signal generating devices made General De Nada's eyes sparkle when he heard what I said about the Inspection Force targeting our fleet. Seeing that, General Say More turned to me and gave me a look that said, "See? He has something in mind."

The Proposal

Two days later, a gravity lens was detected near Jupiter's orbit. It signaled the onset of the sixth battle. At that point, we had no idea that this next battle would be such a critical one. Although I suppose there were signs.

Escorted by the Inspection Force, we deployed our fleet toward the place where the gravity lens had emerged, and each ship slowly changed direction as needed to get into formation. The inertia from our original course of navigation was pushing our fleet in one direction like an enormous current, which meant the ships couldn't easily make an effective change in course. But we tried to maintain spacing and did our best to line up for battle. We intended to attempt something like a preemptive attack the moment the enemy fleet appeared. Not many of us believed it would be successful because it seemed that we were about to get hit on the back of the head by friendly fire. We'd lost our will to fight even before the fight began. I felt like I was on a slave ship or something, and I vowed to myself that I would fight if I'm told to fight but that I wouldn't needlessly risk my life.

Right at that moment, Commander De Nada issued an emergency order throughout the fleet.

"All fleet, stop acceleration and be on standby."

Typically, a directive like this one would be issued through the general staff, but this one came directly from the supreme commander's mouth, which left even the general staff befuddled. Then came the next order: "All assault ships must stop communication and move freely at the discretion of the captains, with a maximum speed of thirty-seven and acceleration below 2.2. Release all decoys and operate them in the same manner as the ships. I repeat, all ships must stop communication, including maneuvering status, until further instructions. Any insubordinate ships will be neutralized without warning."

Chaos ensued. The general had just forfeited the right to command during the fighting. Right before a battle. Nevertheless, when the flagship released the decoys and other ships followed suit, even the Inspection Force ships joined in. They had to. If they didn't follow the order, they would've had no choice but to face Lucifer particles fired from the flagship.

And so we silently drifted around the vastness of outer space at the discretion of the captains of each ship. Some apparently maneuvered following the advice of field staff officers, but I think the majority ended up following the decoys. "Do something freely" is a challenging order. The moment you lower your guard, you end up moving in a pattern. But that wasn't very important anyway. The important thing was that the ships were spreading out in no particular pattern overall.

The Proposal

Just like the other operations officers of the general staff, I had an inkling about General De Nada's intention behind his orders. If you looked at the radar, you could see that as a whole our fleet was spreading out in large circles with the flagship at the center. It was impossible to tell which blips were the actual ships as we were mingled with decoys. Although each ship was moving in pattern-less disarray, the overall movement of the fleet was consistent. We were spreading out like gas molecules into wider and wider spaces, lowering our density.

You're right. We were sinking. Deep into the abyss that was outer space. The lower the density of the fleet, the deeper the universe that surrounded us. And in the middle of that deep, deep space, we waited for the enemy to show up. Because the enemy would appear somewhere near us, no matter where we were. We were going to lie in wait, and when the enemy appeared, we were going to move toward them, increasing our density. From the enemy's perspective, they would be under siege the moment they crossed over to this side of the universe. It might even feel as though the entire universe was closing in on them.

Just like that, we were becoming a galaxy. The way the ships irregularly burned fuel as they drifted resembled a group of stars. A group of stars that were twinkling here and there in peace, drifting without a set pattern or purpose. Once again, we were becoming stars to each other.

Right then, our three-dimensional radar captured something interesting. It detected the Earth fish in our fleet. I'm talking about the Inspection Force ships. They were completely clueless about the order to move "freely." While other ships were drifting and floating in outer space without any rules or patterns, like the space species of fish in the zero-gravity saltwater aquafarm, those Earth species of fish were watching what their kind was doing and ended up in a line, facing one direction. The radar detected the majority of the Inspection Force fleet aiming their weapons at the spot where the gravity lens had appeared and crowding toward one place—around General De Nada's flagship.

Watching them, the captain of the escort ship I was on asked, "What are they doing? All the communication has been cut off, so why are they gathering together like that? Did the general staff practice something like this? Why are they in an attack formation when they're not even going to fight?"

"We never practiced anything like this. The commander's order was a first for even the general staff."

A few moments later, the enemy fleet emerged from the interdimensional portal. They seemed to rearrange their

The Proposal

battle line to face us, but I could tell from their ship placement that they were as confused as we were. They probably knew that about half of our ships were decoys, but I doubted that they could understand the reason our commander decided on the fleet's formation—dense and crowded in the center, scattered and spread out thinly at the outer edge. It was a formation that was not in any tactical manual in the entire universe.

The enemy fleet soon transitioned into a close-knit formation and began to accelerate toward the center of our fleet. It was clear that they had more battle experience than us, and so perhaps they had knowledge about the best course of action in this kind of situation. The enemy ships opened fire and began charging toward General De Nada's flagship as they had done in previous battles. They were charging with such great force, as if they intended to approach our fleet close enough to cancel out the Buggler Paradox and engage in close combat. Seeing what was happening, our ships begin to stir. The center was on the verge of being breached. Yet, no order came from General De Nada's flagship, even though everyone was waiting for it. The order to close in on the enemy on all sides, I mean.

That wasn't all. Far from issuing a siege order, the flagship began accelerating toward the enemy all of a sudden. The general staff was completely bewildered. Close combat is so dangerous that it is rarely, if ever, chosen as a strategy. And we were certainly not in a position to use the flagship as bait. Losing the flagship at that point basically meant losing the entire fleet since we were maneuvering the ships under the supreme commander's order, whose real intention was still incomprehensible.

Even though no order was issued yet, we quickly moved to redirect our ships toward the center of the fleet. Some began to accelerate toward the flagship, and others followed. We didn't need an order at that point, you see.

That was when the strangest thing happened. The Inspection Force's elite ships that had surrounded the flagship began to increase their speed along with the flagship. The Inspection Force—the Inspection Force led by General Liddell who had no intention whatsoever of fighting against the enemy fleet—was at the forefront of the close attack formation and acting as an advance guard.

Why? Because they were ultimately Earth fish. The moment they were ordered to hover freely without a set formation, they lost all sense of balance and began to feel as though they were falling. To counter this feeling, they gathered toward the center. To not lose sight of the flagship. Desperately waiting for someone to issue an order. It didn't matter if the order came from the ringleader of the rebel forces. But since General De Nada didn't issue any orders, even when the enemy began charging at them, they were feeling antsy and impatient. And so when the flagship began to charge at the enemy, it must have seemed like a signal to charge.

Genius! He turned the Inspection Force into the vanguard!

Do you know what the entire scene looked like? An image reflected in a mirror. The Inspection Force and the enemy fleet, all charging toward General De Nada in the center. I wonder if the Inspection Force knew. That there was a huge mirror before them. That if there was a group that put one in mind of the enemy, it wasn't General De Nada and his general staff but General Liddell's Inspection Force Command themselves.

At a mere three light-seconds away from the enemy fleet, General De Nada's flagship opened fire. Only when the flagship had advanced to the point where it couldn't avoid a collision with the enemy fleet despite attempts to slow down as much as possible, General De Nada finally issued an order to the entire fleet.

"Close in and destroy the enemy."

At his command, every ship activated its engines at full throttle and charged at the center of the enemy fleet with explosive momentum. I could feel artificial gravity pulling us back. Here and there, Lucifer particles belched terrifying beams of light at the enemy fleet. Amid all the chaos, we heard General De Nada ordering the Inspection Force to stop the Buggler Maneuver and focus on increasing the accuracy of their gunfire. It meant they were close enough to the enemy ships that the Buggler Paradox was no longer applicable.

The moment I heard his voice, it suddenly struck me why General De Nada hadn't brought me aboard the flagship. He wasn't planning to come out of this battle alive. He wanted to save my life because he had learned what I was going to do after this combat!

However, there was no time for me to be sentimental. Because my eyes caught the tragic sight of both sides' assault squadrons being destroyed by Lucifer particles. Dozens and dozens of ships exploded every minute, but neither side was relenting. Since they'd long gone past the point where they could maneuver the ships to avoid being shot down, the only viable option was to simply attempt to fly through each other.

General De Nada flew straight toward the enemy flagship. The enemy flagship flew at the general's flagship. Escort ships began to flock around them. The situation wasn't unfavorable to our fleet. The warships escorting General De Nada's flagship were mounted with the strongest and best-performing weapons ever invented by humanity. Although they were intended to be aimed at General De Nada in case he became too much of a threat, they were being used for the right reasons at that moment—not to strike our fleet from the back but to penetrate the enemy ranks.

While the rest of our ships were closing in on the enemy from a distance, the first wave of the assault on both sides were now within 0.5 light-seconds from each other. The excessive release of Lucifer particles within such a small area can cause wave interference among the particles, and some ships were now pushing their artillery to the limit, bombarding the enemy with a continuous fire of Lucifer particles beyond what was sustainable, to the point a number of ships ended up overheating and exploding.

That was how General De Nada confronted his fate. Regardless of who was on the enemy flagship, what the Prophet had said, or the true nature of the Temple of the Doom, General De Nada probably concluded that he could only discover the truth, not from rumors, but from seeing everything firsthand. That was his style. After all, he was a field commander, not a politician.

I held my breath. I'm sure everyone did. In the blink of an eye, our fleet penetrated the center of the enemy fleet. Starting where the two fleets overlapped, an enormous fire caught blaze. Then, a colossal explosion occurred. The vast amount of Lucifer particles interfering with each other ended up wiping out the entire area. At the speed of light.

There was no sound. Because there was no air for sound to travel through. Instead, there was a dreadful flash of light. The ultimate flash of light to end all flashes of lights. Aimless Lucifer particles were carried away by that flash of light and scattered in every direction. There wasn't a single ship, whether friend or foe, that could avoid them. Because no ship is faster than light. Soon after, the ships began to explode one after another. The ones closest to the original site of explosion were the first to become purgatory particles. Because even the density of purgatory particles in the area was excessively high, an observation ship issued a warning about secondary explosions from purgatory particles.

Lucifer particles struck the spaceships with a power and intensity that was inversely proportional to the square of the distance from the site of the original explosion. Meaning, the ships that were ten times closer received a blow that was a hundred times stronger. As a result, nearly all of the Inspection Force ships, seventy-two percent of all enemy ships, and seventeen percent of all other friendly ships were incapacitated in a mere 5.47 seconds.

We had lost all communication with the flagship.

10

What happened afterward proceeded somberly one step at a time. In lieu of the commander, the general staff assumed the right to command to use the surviving ships to chase and destroy the scattered enemy ships. In accordance with the Allied Orbital Forces Command's official instructions, and also the instructions penned in *Prophecies*, we took no prisoners. The instructions said that if the Temple of Doom was indeed a gateway in time and space, taking prisoners of war could potentially be sowing the seeds of another disaster.

After everything was wrapped up, the very last order left by General De Nada before the battle commenced was delivered to the general staff. Like it was his last will and testament.

"Once the enemy fleet has been destroyed, change the strategic objective. The ultimate target of our attack is …"

Then came peace at last. A time where we could slowly reflect on ourselves. Or, perhaps, a time where we must inevitably confront ourselves.

11

Everything up to here summarizes what I've experienced so far. I imagine it will differ from the UES's official account.

The Allied Orbital Forces' Investigation Team will be here soon. Oh, actually, not the Investigation Team but the Special Investigations Force. And they will make up a truth that isn't the truth. The story of Commander De Nada of the rebel forces. But you have to believe in me until the very end. No matter what people may call us.

There were some people who said we should return to Earth now that the war was over. But I don't think that's possible. Because the Allied Orbital Forces didn't send us a rescue team but the Special Investigations Force. When I heard that, my heart sank. We knew the composition of their personnel. And how similar they were to the Inspection Force. Above all, we know very well the kind of policies they'd enacted to eliminate us, the space-born humans. So, it's almost certain that the UES, the Prophet's enforcement organization, will brand us as the rebels.

It's also because of the terrifying weapons that are currently in our possession. Since we no longer have an enemy, these weapons will likely be aimed at humanity. The fight has ended, and the weapons should now be tossed away, but if the UES gets their hands on them, they won't do that. Actually, I guess no one would do that. Because these weapons are a source of unassailable, absolute power. That's why I can't return to Earth quite yet.

Of course, there is a way to make sure that the weapons never fall into the wrong hands. We can just lead the fleet to Earth and overthrow the UES for real. No one would be able to stop us. But I don't want to do that. I don't even want to fight. Because the thing that humanity's very first spacecraft fleet wanted to destroy was not a mysterious alien fleet from outer space but the wall of vast distance between the two humanities of Earth-borns and space-borns.

The UES will say something completely different. I don't know what they will say happened, but General De Nada is no longer with us so they can't use him as a scapegoat. He was struck by Lucifer particles and vanished without a trace. The UES will likely say that General De Nada overpowered General Liddell's Inspection Force and planned to lead the

The Proposal

rest of the fleet to Earth. But that's definitely not the truth. Do you know what General De Nada's final order to the general staff was?

"Once the enemy fleet has been destroyed, change the strategic objective. The final target of our attack is the Temple of Doom."

Instead of Earth, he was going to take on the Temple of Doom. That mysterious, colossal celestial body. He probably didn't know exactly how. Still, he was certain about this one thing—regardless of whatever it actually was, the appearance within our solar system of a celestial body with a mass enormous enough to affect the orbit of Jupiter posed a critical threat to the survival of humanity.

But the UES won't share this story. They will simply label what happened as a mutiny. Which leaves us with nowhere to go. And no one to welcome us.

Still, there were people who were determined to return to Earth, so we gathered them together in a small convoy. So that the Special Investigations Force, once they get here, can have them taken back to Earth. The rest of us here respect their decision. Because that might in fact have been the correct path.

I'm entrusting this letter and ring to a colleague who decided to head back to Earth. The ring was made by the best zero-gravity jeweler in the entire universe. The shop has since closed down forever, so you won't be able to find anything like it anywhere else. I'm sorry that I can't be there to put the ring on your finger myself. General De Nada saved my life to do just that; sadly, I'll be disappointing him too.

After the war ended, I was going to ask you to marry me. If you didn't want to live in zero-gravity, I would've gone to live on Earth. Under just one condition—that you don't force me to travel until my bone density increased. It would've been enough for me if you promised that we would go on orbital trips occasionally after our baby was born. We wouldn't have needed to show spacecrafts to the baby, but I really wanted to show them the zero-gravity sea. Now, it seems that I won't be able to say this to you in person.

We plan to fly toward the Temple of Doom soon. I don't know what lies beyond there. It could be another universe, another time, or just the other side of the same universe. If I go through, will I eventually cross over again to this side and attack General De Nada in the past? In that way, I might end up trapped in time forever.

No, I don't think that will be the case. Because that was De Nada's fate—a prophecy that he broke himself. But perhaps in that moment our destinies were switched. And now, this has become my fate. Not his.

The Proposal

I remember the look on General De Nada's face the very first time I showed him the Temple of Doom. The way he peered intently into the gravity lens. His intense gaze that seemed to suck everything in. Right, this is not something to be feared at all. It's the same universe anyway, here and there. I should go and do whatever I can. Although I can't predict what will happen.

I promise I'll be back. Isn't it strange? That a space-born like me thinks about returning somewhere.

Now I have a home too. It's where you are. Thanks. And goodbye.

I'll be your shining star on the other side of the universe.

honfordstar.com